CALL TO ARMS: CAPERNICA

VETERAN

Colonel Jonathan P. Brazee, USMC (Ret)

A Semper Fi Press Book

Copyright © 2019 Jonathan Brazee

ISBN-13: 978-1-945743-36-8
(Semper Fi Press)

Printed in the United States of America

This is a work of fiction. All of the characters, names, incidents, organizations, and dialogue in this novel are either the products of the author's imagination or are used fictitiously.

Acknowledgements:
I want to thank all those who took the time to pre-read this book, catching my mistakes in both content and typing. I want to thank Kelly O'Donnell, James Caplan, and Micky Cocker. Any remaining typos and inaccuracies are solely my fault.

Original Cover Art by Almaz Sharipov

DEDICATION

Dedicated to Colonel Rick Rescorla, US Army (Ret)

Awarded the Silver Star and Purple Heart for Actions in
Vietnam

Awarded the Presidential Citizens Medal for Extraordinary
Sacrifice for Saving Countless Lives During the Attack on the
Twin Towers, 11 September 2001, at the Cost of His Own Life

Chapter 1

War came to Capernica on a beautiful Landing Day.

Master Sergeant Lester Baptiste Arceneaux, Army of the Confederation, (Retired), pulled his Ion-6 in front of the little one-story house he shared with his wife. Emmeline was standing on the porch, silently watching him, a wisp of gray hair loose from the tight bun she normally wore fluttering in front of her face. After 46 years of marriage, he knew that wasn't a good sign. She was not happy with him.

"You know, you can still come, Em," he said. "We can catch a river bus."

She rolled her eyes, pushed the loose wisp of hair back, and said, "Right. So, I can sit and watch you tell war stories to all your VSW *saleau* while you get drunk. No, you go have your fun and leave me be."

Les felt guilty that he was relieved she said no—which was probably her intent from the beginning. He loved his wife dearly. How could he not? She was still the raven-haired beauty who married the broke private first class, then followed him from one shithole post to another, never complaining, always supporting. Sure, her hair was more gray now than black, but so was his beard.

If she'd asked, he'd have taken her to Red Rocks, which would have put a damper on meeting up with his buddies, the old soldiers and sailors who'd retired to scattered locations across the Grande Isle. Most were centered around San Isabella down the river, but after Juan dela Cort passed last year, Les was the only retired military man or woman in Fox. Landing Day might be a patriotic celebration honoring the first humans to set foot on Capernica, but to Les, it was when he could meet up with his tribe. With Emmeline there, he'd be concerned about her being bored, and in the end, they'd cut the evening short and head back home.

For a moment, he thought he should push her. There would be plenty to see at Red Rocks, more than just sitting alone at home, but she'd made her choice not to get in the way of his fun. And that was just one more reason that he loved her.

"Make sure you take a Sober-Up before you ride home, *vieux*," she said with a slight frown. "You didn't survive all those wars just to end up head-first into a tree because you were *pieyied*."

Les hid his smile—that would even get her more pissed at him. After so many years in the service, he'd lost most of the Cajun phrases from back on Pontchartrain. When Emmeline was angry or stressed, the old words tended to make their appearances.

He just nodded instead, slipped down his visor, then clamped his prosthetic hand on the throttle and gunned the Ion. With a surge of silent power that always excited him, the big bike picked up speed. The Ion was his pride and joy. It was old, bought when he retired and arrived on Capernica, but then again, so was he. An old bike for an old man. Some of the young folks of the town made fun of it, used to the throwaway culture of their generation, but the Ion-6 was made to last. It purred just the same as when it was brand new.

The road to south from Fox was new, only five years old. Most heavy traffic still went by river, but a man couldn't scream down the road at 120 KPH onboard a river bus. The bike could hit 270, but not on the San Isabella Highway, and he'd promised Emmeline to keep it at 120.

With the celebration at Red Rocks, the two-lane highway was packed, so even after coming down Novak Pass, 120 was out of the question today. It was nothing like what would be between San Isabella and the other river communities, where even with an extra two lanes, traffic would be at a crawl. There were times when Les wished they'd retired to the provincial capital instead of Fox—retired master sergeants were not awash in retired pay, and at least in Fox, he was able to buy a real, if small, house—but for today, he was glad as he wove through the hovers.

Forty-five minutes after coming down the pass, he reached Red Rocks. He checked his wristcomp and made a friend-query. He was early, and no one else had arrived yet, not even Major Uffa. The serious drinking wouldn't start until later in the afternoon, but the major never let the time of day stop her, and she was usually the first to arrive at any get-together.

He swung his leg off the Ion, gave it a pat with his organic hand, then wandered into the celebration. As expected, it was packed, mostly with families at this time of day. That was OK with him. He enjoyed people-watching, especially children. He and Emmeline never had children, much to their chagrin. It had never happened naturally, and the Army wouldn't pay for IVF or creche-bred-children while the soldier was on active duty—and by the time Les retired, they were past the age limit for either of those methods. Some people his age thought that the screeches of children were annoying, but they filled him with joy . . . and more than a little sadness that he and Emmeline would never have any. As they said, children were the future.

With the war going on, he'd wondered if the crowds would be smaller, but if anything, they were larger. The war might not have made much of a direct impact on Capernica, as far out in the arm as it was, but it was hard to ignore the reports on the news. And there were some direct impacts, personal losses. The province had lost over 50 sons and daughters so far. Even in Fox, Mattie and Nic's girl Jinny had been killed two months before when her corvette was lost. From the looks of it, people needed the mental break.

Show your patriotism, eat terribly unhealthy food, and ride the midway seemed like a good way to do that.

And drink, of course.

Time to get a leg up on that.

It might be early, but that didn't faze a master sergeant. He started to make his way through the food stalls and back to the beer tents when the aroma of fried foods assaulted his nose, and his stomach growled in response.

Better get something in my belly before I start drinking.

He stood with his hands on his hips, surveying the scene. It was lunchtime, and lines were long around most of the stands. He thought about a redburger, but that line was longer than most. The fried butter line was shorter. Even for his cast-iron stomach, that was a little much, and he realized he might be making a mistake to eat that and then drown it with beer, but the soldier in him rose to the challenge, and he joined the back of the line.

His hand drifted to his bright red "Retired Master Sergeant, Confederation Army" ballcap, straightening it out so it would be noticed. He never asked for a military discount, but he'd never turn one down if offered.

The next stand over was a mist-candy, something Les couldn't abide. It was pure sugar, too light even to bite. There were a young man and a little girl at the front of the line getting served.

Cute girl, Les thought, and he felt a pang of jealousy watching the young man, wondering who he was. He looked a little young to be a father, but these days, who knows?

"Don't tell mom I gave it to you," the young man said, handing the girl a stick of candy.

So, brother it is.

"Ah, spoiling the little one," the girl behind the counter said.

She dipped another stick into the barrel, charging it as the candy particles swirled to cover it. She leaned over and handed it to the girl, saying, "Here you go. For later."

"Can you move up, old man?" someone said behind him.

Two people had already been served their fried butter, and Les was now second in line. He turned back where another young man, this one with one arm insolently around a young woman's shoulders, stared at him.

For a moment, Les was tempted to give the young punk a shove. Nothing too hard, but enough to teach him some manners.

I'll show you old man, youngster.

But he *was* an old man, and he hadn't been paying attention. He took a deep breath, then closed the gap with the people in front of him before looking back at the little girl and her brother.

The young man had started to swipe his wristcomp to pay for the mistcandy when the woman behind the counter said, "My treat. She reminds me of my little sister."

"Uh . . . thank you," the young man replied flustered. "Lynda, thank the lady."

"Thank you," the little girl mumbled, her face already buried in the mist-candy.

Come on, kid. She's giving you an opening. Take it.

But the guy just gaped at the woman who was waiting expectantly for him to say something.

Clearly not Army material, Les thought.

"Are you done?" another woman asked, tapping the guy on the shoulder.

The woman was an Army second lieutenant in her Charlies, and somehow, Les had missed that, so focused was he on the little drama taking place.

Damn, old man. Great situational awareness there.

The brother and sister left, and the lieutenant stepped forward, the shoulder tabs indicating that she was a logistics officer.

"What can I get you?" the girl behind the counter asked.

"A double, with gold flakes," the lieutenant said.

Les felt a nudge from behind. He turned, and the young kid, arm still around the girl, stared defiantly at him. The girl had an excited look in her eyes as she looked at him, as if waiting for something to happen.

"You're up, so, how about you order and get the fuck out of the way."

Les started to cock back his prosthetic hand. One shot, and the kid would crumple to the dirt.

Not worth it. Let him live.

"That will be three unis, ma'am," the mistcandy girl said from the next stand.

"Take my place," Les said suddenly, ignoring the kid's less-than-polite comment and stepping to the mistcandy stand just at the lieutenant raised her wristcomp to pay.

"I've got that, Lieutenant. *Vigilamus pro te,*" he said.

The lieutenant looked at him in surprise and responded, "*Vigilamus pro te.* Thank you, sir."

Oh, my gosh, she's really a boot, he thought, before saying, "I weren't no officer, ma'am. Made master sergeant before I lost this to a pirate in the Avon Sector."

He lifted his right arm and rapped it against the edge of the counter.

"You were a grunt?" the lieutenant asked.

"Yes, ma'am. Proud of it. And you? Just finish OCS?" he asked, pointing to her chest that was painfully void of ribbons.

"Logistics school. I'm heading to Interpolative Planning School on Braxton in another week, so I came home for Landing Day. After I graduate and report in to my new unit, I may not be able to come home for the duration."

"Braxton? We've got bases there?" Les asked, surprised. That was something new to him. Braxton was a newly terraformed planet, farther out on the arm and without much in the way of military installations, as far as he knew.

"Temporary. Some of the schools moved out there from the core what with the war. Uh . . . do you want one?" the lieutenant said, lifting her mist-candy.

That crap? Good God, no.

"No, thanks. I just saw you in line and wanted to pay for it."

She seemed to think for a moment, then asked, "How about a beer then? It would be my honor."

"Now, you're speaking my language, Lieutenant," Les said with a smile and holding out his prosthetic hand. "Master Sergeant Lester Arceneaux, Army of the Confederation, Retired."

"Second Lieutenant Wysoki," she said, shaking his hand. "Cel Wysoki."

She flinched, ever-so-slightly at his touch. Les was used to it. Most people had their limbs regrown, but the process was long and painful. Les had wanted to get back to his unit ASAP after losing his arm, so he'd agreed to accept a prosthetic, intending on getting a real one regrown later. Only later never came, and once retired . . . well, the Army didn't care so much for their welfare of ex-soldiers. He'd never gotten the procedure approved. To be more accurate, he was now on a VA waiting list and had been since he retired . . . and with no end date in sight.

"I know just the place. Same beer tent for the last fifty-some-odd years," Les said.

It was also the place where he'd be meeting up with his VSW mates, so he could commandeer a table and wait for them to arrive.

"One thing I learned, ma'am, when I was in the Big A, was that a soldier never, and I mean never, turns down a beer," he added.

The lieutenant laughed and was about to say something when a clap reverberated across the sky. Les recognized the sound, and his heart dropped. He looked up, spotting what he'd expected.

He grabbed the lieutenant by the arm and said, "You'd better report in, ma'am."

"But I don't have a unit here. I'm on leave."

"I think your leave's been canceled. Unless I miss my guess, those are Wolvic landing craft."

He didn't know why he said, "Unless I miss my guess." There was no doubt about it.

Jonathan P. Brazee

The lieutenant, looking awfully young, stood there with confusion written across her face. He realized she had no idea what to do.

"Those're Wolvic landing craft, and that means we're under attack, ma'am. You need to report in."

"But to who? I'm in transit between schools," she said, dropping her candy to the ground.

Good question. Where should she go? With the Wolvics landing, she wasn't about to get to Pryce and the planetary headquarters. Out here in on the Grand Isle, that left San Isabella and Lassiter. He gave her a hard once-over. She was a boot POG, not even trained, and maybe the closest would be best.

"There's the recruiting station in San Isabella. "They should be able to get a message out for you."

The lieutenant looked to the south to where the streaks of smoke were converging. On San Isabella, no doubt, and he's just suggested she head into what was undoubtedly going to be a dicey situation.

Bad advice, old man.

"Your other choice would be to get to Camp Lassiter. That would be the closest installation."

With the Wolvics converging on San Isabella, Camp Lassiter, the small garrison located in Miguel Pass, some 100 or so kilometers to the northwest, was probably a better choice. The way there might remain clear, and while the Three-oh-fifty-first was a composite battalion, at least they had some combat capability.

"I think I'll try for the recruiting station," she said. "It's not far from my family's home."

"You have a way to get there?"

"Yeah. I've got my brother's Lighting."

Nice ride. Her brother must have some cash.

He grabbed her upper arm and said, "Give it a shot, if you think that's best, ma'am. But if there's fighting, don't push it. Turn your brother's hover around and get to the garrison.

"You think there's going to be fighting in the streets?"

"The Wolvics didn't come for afternoon tea, ma'am. And most of those are landing craft, not fighters."

She looked back to the landing craft as they descended in the south, started to pull away, then stopped and asked, "What about you? Are you going to be OK?"

"I'll make my way back to Fox," he said.

The lieutenant held out her and to shake his and said, "You be careful getting up there."

"I'll be OK. No one's going to bother a one-armed old fart like me. *Vigilamus pro te,* Lieutenant."

"*Vigilamus pro te,*" she replied before turning and hurrying off.

"God's speed, Lieutenant," he muttered, watching her for a moment as she wound her way through the crowd.

For a moment, he'd had a strong desire to go with her and make sure she got to where she needed to be. One of the most important missions a SNCO had was to train the junior officers, and that instinct was still strong in him. If he was still on active duty, he'd have taken her under his wing, but he hadn't been in uniform for years. He was just an old vet, with a wife waiting for him at home.

The thought of Emmeline spurred him into action. Most of the people were gawking at the sky, some even clapping their hands in appreciation, thinking they were part of a show, probably. But the Capernican Air Guard didn't have landing craft like that. A few people were looking concerned, and even fewer still were starting to move out. Les knew that wouldn't last long, and he didn't want to be caught in a panicking crowd. He wound his way through the people to where he'd parked his bike in the north lot.

His big Ion, jet black with orange trim, towered over the other bikes, but some asshole had parked their little bright silver Race Crown directly behind it, blocking the way. Les stood over the small bike for a moment. It was part of the bike culture that no one touched another's bike, even a toy like a Race Crown, but then again, it was also bike culture not to be a dick and block someone else in. The front wheel of the Race Crown was locked, but the thing couldn't weigh more than 70 kilos, so Les bent over to hook his arms under the handlebars when an explosion reverberated from the direction of the fairgrounds, the concussion making his ears pop. He spun around to where smoke was rising over the trees. The sounds of screams reached him, and a moment later, his wristcomp went off in a warning.

He didn't need to look. It would be telling him to either shelter in place or go home, and if he didn't look, he could assume it was the second.

Unless he should go see what happened. Soldiers ran to the sound of gunfire, something that had been ingrained in him. But then again, he wasn't a soldier anymore. The fairgrounds had been hit by aircraft or from orbit, and there wasn't much he could do about it either. There would be police and medical personnel who'd be responding, and he'd probably just be in the way if he tried to help.

He had to get home.

All niceties aside, he kicked over the silver Race Crown, then started his Ion-6. Power pulsed through it, making his thighs vibrate. He backed it up, bouncing it over the prone Race Crown, then fed the power as he raced through the lot.

He was one of the first to reach the road, but hovers were still streaming in. Many were stopped, the drivers stepping out to see what was going on, but others attempted to bypass them and get to Red Rocks.

"Turn back!" Les shouted. "Do not proceed!"

He was roundly ignored.

If he were in a hover, he'd have been trapped, but he wended his way through the mass of incoming traffic. People tried to stop him to find out what was happening, but he just yelled at them to turn around and get back home. They had wristcomps, and they could read them just as easily as he could.

Les gave his a glance, realizing that he should call Emmeline and tell her he was on his way, but the top line was now grayed out.

Of course, he berated himself. *The Wolvics would be jamming the signal.*

After that, he was a little more forthcoming, telling them there had been an attack, and they were to return home to await further instructions. All of this took time, time he should have been using to get home. Fox was still another 60 klicks north, and at this rate, it was going to take him hours to make the trip, hours where Emmeline would be worried sick.

If he even made it home. He'd been in enough wars to know that fighting had a way of closing off travel. He wanted—no, he *needed*—to be back before that happened.

He heard no more explosions as he distanced himself from Red Rocks, but twice, he heard the sounds of aircraft. He couldn't see them, and he'd been out of the loop so long that he couldn't identify whether they were Wolvic, Capernican, or Confederation by ear. Back in the day, he could. Back in the day, however, he was young, dumb, and full of cum, as they say, ready to take on the galaxy. Now he was just an old man trying to get home to his wife.

But his Ion was still a kickass bike. As he got farther down the road, there were fewer vehicles, and he started to increase the power, weaving in and out as he blasted down the road. Some hovers were still heading in, and they honked at him as he swerved by them, sometimes riding up on the shoulder. Others had already managed to turn around and were heading back. Les blew by them as if they were standing still. He thought Emmeline would forgive him for exceeding his promised 120 KPH limit.

The smell hit him before the curve in the road, a smell that awoke his lizard brain, something too deeply embedded to ever forget, and he automatically slowed down. Death and destruction were ahead of him. Even slowed, he was barely able to avoid the wreckage on the highway. A handful of hovers were strewn like broken toys across the road. For a moment, he thought the Wolvics had bombed the road, and rage began to burn inside of him. But then he took in the gouge that took down trees and tore up the road. Something had hit the highway, and hit hard. More wreckage, all in small pieces, littered the impact site. He couldn't even tell what it had been. He hoped it was a Wolvic landing craft, but he feared it had been a Capernican Air Guard plane, which would have been the first to scramble and wouldn't be much of a match for a Wolvic gunship in orbit overhead.

He slowed to a stop. It was one thing to leave Red Rocks where there were first responders to attend to the wounded, but this was different. There was no one else. He set the parking gyros and stepped off his bike, already knowing what he would find. Once smelled, death was never mistaken for something else.

On the far side of the zone of destruction, a Chevy People Mover was stopped, a woman standing in shock as he looked over the scene. Les could see at least four children inside, looking out the front windshield.

"Ma'am, just take your kids and get out of here," Les yelled.

"Is anybody hurt?" the woman yelled back.

Can't you see the mangled hovers, lady? And what do you think that lump is right in front of you?

"I've got this, ma'am. Your kids, they don't need to see any of this." She looked uncertain, so he yelled again, "I've got this."

The woman looked around one more time, and it looked like she finally realized that there was a burnt body not five meters from her. She blanched, then got back in the Chevy and started backing up.

Les stepped onto the torn-up highway. There were the remains of three, maybe four hovers scattered on and off the road. Among the pieces were body parts. Les couldn't help them, so he kept moving. A Blackstone SUV was on its side, but mostly whole, and if anyone survived this, it would be in that one.

As he made his way to it, he wondered what had happened. The more bits and pieces he saw, the more he thought it had been a Capernican Air Guard plane that has caused this. Had the pilot been hit and tried to land on the road? Or was is just shitty luck that it had been shot down and crashed here? Either way, the people in the hovers, all just planning to celebrate another Landing Day, were dead.

He was vaguely aware of more vehicles coming up behind him as he walked the last few steps to the Blackstone. A male body was crumpled up against the windshield, twisted in a way that human's backs don't twist. Behind him, however, a pair of wide eyes stared out at him.

"It's OK. I've got you," he reassured the young teen, reaching over to pull on the passenger door that wouldn't budge.

Only how the hell do I get to her?

"Are you all right?" he asked as he tried to figure out what to do.

The teen didn't respond.

He gave the door another tug. The body of the SUV was damaged, but the frame didn't look warped. He wasn't sure why the door wouldn't open.

Unless . . .

"Look, honey. Is your door locked?"

She just looked at him.

"I want to get you out of there, but you need to reach out and open the door."

Finally, she responded, reaching out a hand before pulling it back.

"Come on, honey, just unlock it. I'll get you out of there."

The teen slowly reached out and waved her hand over the release before yanking it back. It was enough, though, and the door unlocked.

Les pulled himself up on the side of the car and pulled open the door. The girl gave a little squeak of alarm, but she didn't try and retreat as he got on his belly and reached down for her. Once his hand brushed her shoulder, she almost jumped forward, grabbing Les in a death grip. Les struggled to gain purchase, his legs dangling in the air, but he managed to pull her out and onto the ground.

He'd assumed she was a teen, but now that he saw her size, if she was a teen, she was only just.

"Hey, do you need any help?" a man shouted from where he'd parked his Ion.

Les gave the rest of the SUV a quick glance. The man in the front, probably this girl's father, was dead, and there was no one else inside. There wasn't another intact, or mostly intact, hover. This girl was probably the only survivor of the crash.

"I'm coming," Les shouted back.

He led the trembling and still silent girl to the waiting man, who'd been joined by a woman.

"Let me have her," the woman said, quickly taking charge. She took the girl back to their hover as the man and Les searched for more survivors. It was a hopeless task, Les knew, but they still had to look.

By the time the two had returned, more hovers had arrived, and people were milling about. An agitated young man in a Scorpion didn't want to wait, and he maneuvered his low-slung fossil-fueled sports car around the wreckage until he reached the other side and roared off in a cloud of black smoke.

"If he can make it with that low clearance, all these hovers should be able to," Les told the other man as they stood next to his car. "How far are you going?"

"Tule," he said, mentioning a town at the end of the road, another 80 klicks past Fox.

"I'd get going, if I were you. No telling if the road's going to remain clear."

"Taylor, come on," the woman said from inside the hover. "She's from Listeville. That's her dad over there, and we need to take her home."

Listeville was the next river town up from Fox, and it would be on the way for them.

"What about, you know, her father?" the man asked.

The girl's father was the only body that wasn't either burnt or torn into tiny pieces. The couple could take the body, but he wasn't sure that would be a good idea given the girl's condition. Les guessed he could try and strap the body to the back of his bike, but that didn't seem like a good choice, either.

He was saved when another driver offered to carry the man's body to Listeville. The couple with the girl took off, their high-clearance hover having little problem getting through the crash site while Les and three others went to retrieve the body.

It never got easy. Les had seen soldiers die. He'd spent almost 35 hours in a foxhole with a dead lieutenant once, and he'd lost too many friends over the years, but he'd never gotten used to corpses as so many of his contemporaries had done. He kept thinking that the body had just been a living, breathing person with a lifetime of memories and loved ones. People assumed he'd gotten beyond that, but they'd assumed wrong.

Still, he had it better than the others, and they dragged the man out of the Blackstone. They dropped him getting him off the side of the car, his head hitting the dirt with a thunk, and one of the others, a young man not much out of his teens, puked. He kept apologizing as they manhandled the limp body back to the truck that was going to transport him home.

Les knew that Emmeline would be at wit's end, so he quickly detached himself and got back on his bike. His wife was a strong woman—she had to be with him being deployed so often while on active duty. But she worried about him, and without him able to call her, she would be assuming the worst. He couldn't put her through that.

The road north of the plane crash was mostly clear, and the big bike barely hesitated as he hit 180 KPH before he backed off to 150. It would do Emmeline any good if he crashed and killed himself a couple of klicks from home.

He passed Pine Rapids, driving too fast and ignoring the questions yelled out to him. From Pine Rapids, Les started climbing, one curve after the other as the road hugged the terrain. He had to slow down or risk going off the cliff. Twenty minutes later, he reached Novak Pass, where the sight of the Green River stretching for kilometers normally made him stop and look. Not this time. He started down Piermont

Grade, and after the fourth switchback, Fox sprawled out below him. He sighed with relief, as he'd half-expected to see Wolvics attacking. The town wasn't huge, but with over three thousand residents, it was the biggest town on the river north of San Isabella and the surrounding suburbs. The provincial capital, Camp Lassiter, and Crystal Bay to the south would be the Wolvic's center of gravity, but with a road and the river, Fox would be on the Wolvics' radar sooner rather than later.

He pulled into the town. People were outside, gathered in groups. A few people saw him and called out, but he had one destination. He pulled into the dirt drive in front of his small brown house and stopped the bike under the huge sycamore tree in the front yard. He'd just engaged the parking gyro when a missile burst out of the front door and hit him in the chest.

"I couldn't reach you, Boo. I kept trying. I thought, I thought . . ." his wife cried into his chest, hot tears soaking through his shirt.

"I know, Em, I know," he said, hugging her tightly. "But I'm here now, and we're going to get through this together. I'm not going to leave you."

Chapter 2

"So, what the hell are we supposed to do?" Glyn Goetze shouted, pounding the table for emphasis. "The Confed fucks aren't doing shit while San Isabella is being taken down. Do any of you think they give a fuck about Fox?"

She glared at the thirty or so others who'd gathered at Leon's, the biggest pub in the town. Glyn was one of the first residents to settle in Fox, some 40 years back, and she'd always mistaken that seniority as authority. Right now, her eyes were on fire with the force of those who are convinced of their righteous opinions.

The question was a valid one, even if Les didn't agree with the premise. Most of the Confederation forces were engaged farther in the spiral arm, and there weren't enough forces on the planet to offer more than a token resistance. But the Confederation couldn't afford to give the Wolvics a foothold this far out on the arm. They would have to react.

Les thought that was probably the Wolvic's mission. They couldn't believe that they could hold Capernica, but they could draw Confed forces away from the main battle areas. Not just for Capernica, but that meant that Ransome, White Mountain, DDK, and Sunshine IV, to name a few, were just as vulnerable. Protecting each of those planets would take a lot more forces than the Wolvics needed to threaten them.

Maybe the generals and admirals had a different view, and Les had never gone to all those high-level officer schools that taught strategy, but master sergeants tended to be practical, above all else. And to him, it just made sense.

The Confederation would respond, but how long would that take, and how much could the Wolvics accomplish before that? He doubted they'd slaughter the entire civilian population wholesale—Les had fought alongside the Wolvics 34 years before against the Reavers during the Sesame Action, and they weren't demons who feasted on human blood. They weren't much different from Confederation troops, to be honest. But civilians would die. That was the nature of war. And infrastructure would be destroyed. Resources would have to be expended to repair the damage.

If the Confederation even deemed it worth the effort. Capernica had been cleared for colonization only fifty-six years before, and it was hardly an economic powerhouse. It was still in Phase 3, with infrastructure still being built. That was one of the reasons that Les and Emmeline had decided to settle there. Neither wanted to return to Pontchartrain or to a tiny apartment on Proclyn, where they'd spent half of Les' time in the army, and Capernica was settled enough so that they wouldn't have to live off the land, yet still open enough that the colonization fee was minimal.

The Confederation Navy and Army would take the planet back, but they might just abandon it afterward.

"Now, Glyn, you know they care about us," Leon—of Leon's Pub—said. "They'll be here."

"When? When we've all been killed?" she asked. "I'll tell you this, I'm not just gonna sit here and let the Wolvic fucks take Fox. I was the first one to homestead here, long before most of you were even a gleam in your fathers' eyes."

"You can always join the others, Glyn. Jack Terrance is down at the docks, getting a group together."

Jack was one of the newer residents, and he'd been gathering volunteers to go help fight the Wolvics. Les didn't know how many had joined him so far, but there had been quite a few milling around the town dock when he and Emmeline passed them on the way to the pub. Les hadn't bothered to ask where they planned on going. He should have stopped and told them to hold fast, someone from the Army would be by within a couple of days, and just heading off for Camp Lassiter or down the river without any guidance was a recipe for disaster.

"I'd go if they'd take me," Glyn said. "Back in Twenty-four, I sure joined the militia when the Posy brothers attacked. I kicked ass then, and I'd kick ass now."

With a huge force of will, Les restrained from rolling his eyes. He'd heard the story a thousand times if he'd heard it once. Maybe Glyn had joined the other villagers back in the day when the Posy Brothers had landed, back when the river was the only way to reach Fox, but from the records Les had finally been goosed into checking, the infamous crew had not yet created their pirate persona of fame. They'd landed their ship at the edge of the town (their drives killing off the trees and creating what was now the town's "Victory Commons"), wanting resupply of food and water. The residents, eager to make a few unis, had agreed, only to be surprised when the crew refused to pay after the delivery. According to Glyn and Horon Weis, the town "militia" had driven the brothers and their crew off. From what Les had gleaned from the records, the ship had indeed departed, but with the food and water onboard and unpaid for.

"I don't hear nobody speaking up," Glyn said. "What, are you all a bunch of pussies? We need a plan to push back the Wolvics when they come."

Les opened his mouth to speak, and Emmeline jabbed an elbow into his ribs. The two of them kept a low profile in the town, keeping out of the spotlight. People knew he was retired Army, but that didn't seem to make much of an impact among the residents.

"I need to say this before they go off on some fool expedition," he whispered to her before speaking up. "The Army, or at least contact teams, will be here. I'd suggest that everyone just hang tight until then."

"And how the fuck do you—" Glyn started, then cutting it off after turning around and seeing who had spoken up. "Oh. Les. What do you mean?"

Les was uncomfortable with all the eyes that locked onto him. He wasn't a shy man—no one made master sergeant if they were. But he'd gotten out of the habit of speaking in front of groups over the years.

"There are contingency plans for all Army units, and that includes up at Camp Lassiter. In a case like this, teams will go out into the towns and organize resistance, if need be, take care of logistics if need be. Whatever's needed."

"That's what I'm talking about, Les! See?" Glyn turned to address the rest. "Maybe the Army isn't going to leave us out to dry.

"How many in a team?" she asked Les, her eyes now beaming.

"How many? Usually, three."

Her eyes darkened again, and she said, "Three. As in one . . . two . . . three? Give me a fucking break! What the hell are three mudhogs going to do for us?"

Les didn't correct the "mudhogs" comment. Mudhogs were infantry, and the **Three-oh-fifty-first** at Lassiter was a composite battalion. The contact teams could be from any branch.

"If we're listed for a team, they'll help organize us for what we need to do. That might be to defend Fox."

"With what? Our hands?" Miguel Dancer asked.

"They'll arm us. Train us up," Les said.

He wasn't totally onboard with the concept. A soldier was a soldier through years of training, and there was no way in hell that civilians could be trained up in a day or two. All they'd be was cannon fodder to hopefully delay the Wolvics until the real Army made planetfall and could take over the fight. Sure, there were exceptions, like that Keen woman on Stanley who'd been in the news, but that was the exception rather than the rule. The real statistics were that these citizen militias suffered tremendous casualty rates when facing professional armies.

Les realized that he was probably biased, but he couldn't help his feelings. Civilians were to be protected, not sacrificed.

He looked around the pub. Several of them, including Glyn, seemed excited by the idea. Quite a few of the others looked apprehensive, as if they wanted nothing to do with fighting. That didn't surprise him. None of them were Capernican natives, all having arrived as immigrants. Landing

Day festivities aside, patriotism didn't have a long history, especially here in Fox where until ten years or so ago, there were fewer than 200 people in the town.

"Isn't that what Terrance is doing right now, getting volunteers?" Tilla Knowles asked.

"We can't just leave it to Jack and the rest who join him," Glyn argued. "When the Wolvics come, they're not gonna let the rest of us be."

The impromptu meeting devolved into a trashpile of arguments and counter-arguments. Another ten minutes was all Les could take, and with a nod to Emmeline, the two left. He was happy to get out into the night air, clean and crisp this far upriver.

Emmeline braided her arm into his as they walked. Small groups were out on porches and corners. Without connectivity, no one knew what was happening, and theories were running rampant.

"Tilla's right, you know," Emmeline said as they walked.

"Right? About what?"

"You know darned well what, Baptiste," she chided, squeezing his arm.

This was serious. Emmeline only called him by his middle name when she was angry or serious about something.

He couldn't hold back the sigh. He'd promised her that when he retired, he'd have nothing to do with the Army anymore, focusing his time and efforts on the two of them. He owed her that after years of leaving her alone while he deployed around the galaxy. She'd relented with the VGW, but that was just old soldiers and sailors telling war stories over steins of beer, no different than her meeting up with Tilla and the others to play Sheaves. It was socializing, nothing more.

But he'd be lying if he didn't feel the siren's call of duty. Physically, he was long past the rigors of soldiering, but his mind hadn't changed--well, if he didn't count the occasional lapses of memory, at least. The same drive that caused him to enlist, seasoned by years in uniform, was still there, and he longed to answer the call.

But he'd promised.

They turned into their small home. It wasn't much, but it was enough. Their life was enough, their golden years together. He gave Emmeline a kiss on the forehead, then sat in his overstuffed chair. His hand automatically went to the remote, ready to turn on the screen, but with a rueful grin, he stopped. All connectivity was gone.

He could hear Emmeline bustling in the kitchen getting their evening tea ready, a ritual Les had come to love. He thought about going in to help, but his wife was protective of the kitchen, and she'd probably chase him out.

The living room was small, about four meters by two. The screen, a 120 cm base-projection, was another of Les' pride and joys, and it took up the center of the room. Around it, the entire wall was covered with flats and holos of their lives together. Plaques from each of his units and copies of promotion warrants and awards filled the left-side "I Love Me" wall. Taking center place on the wall was his old ME2 MEW, mounted in a case.

Emmeline called the room, specifically his wall, a "cathedral to dead memories," but she never objected.

His eyes locked onto the MEW. Technically, "MEW" supposedly stood for "Meson Energy Weapon," but to the soldiers who had ever carried them, they were fondly called "Mother Effing Whipass." Most people who'd seen his assumed it was a model, but it was the real thing, the actual weapon he'd used in combat. Defanged, now, without the syn-module, but the real deal. Les' last unit was also one of the last three battalions to still have the Winchester-Leung meson-beam weapon in their Table of Equipment, and as an "old corps" master sergeant, Les had insisted in carrying the heavy weapon while most others had eagerly taken the new generation of field weapons—lighter dart-throwers, for the most part. The MEW might have its flaws—OK, it did have its many flaws—but when it hit, it packed a powerful punch. But with them being phased out, Les had filled out a Special Request Form-2 to keep his weapon upon his retirement. To his surprise, the request had been approved, the syn-module removed, and he was presented the mounted weapon at his ceremony.

The old beamer had saved his ass on more than a few occasions, and when Emmeline wasn't looking, he had a habit of standing in front of it, stroking the stock. He had a sudden urge to do that now, but Emmeline would be back at any moment. He didn't want her to think he was crazy.

He'd dedicated his life to the Army, but now it was time to let others pick up the banner and carry on. The Army didn't need old men like him. He needed to let go.

But he couldn't, he realized with a start, standing up. He might not be ready to put the uniform back on, but he still had a duty to the Confederation and to the Army.

"Hold my tea for me," he said, poking his head in the kitchen.

"Why," his wife asked warily, her eyes tightening.

"I've got to go find Jack Temperance," he said.

"Baptiste Arceneaux," she started, pushing the teapot aside. "There's no way in hell I'm going to let you volunteer—"

"Hush, Em. I'm not going to join up with them," he interrupted.

"Then what are you going to do?"

"Those young fools will probably jump in a boat and go downriver. Get themselves killed. No, they need to stay here and wait. Like I said, the contact teams will be here by-and-by, and they can get Jack and the rest to where they can actually do something."

Emmeline stood there, hands on her hips as she weighed what he was saying.

"I promise. I'm not going with them. I'm just going to get them not to go off half-cocked and get themselves killed."

She waited a few more moments, then said, "OK, you go do that. But I want you back in thirty-minutes, no more than that."

He rushed forward and gave her a kiss on the cheek before he spun around, afraid that the youngsters might have already left.

"Thirty minutes, Baptiste," she shouted after him. "I'll keep your tea warm."

Chapter 3

Les shouldn't have worried about Jack and his group. The enthusiasm was there, but not the concept of how to meet up with Confederation forces. Jack, a 30-something new resident who'd moved into Fox just two years prior, seemed relieved when Les had told him to wait for official guidance, and late the next afternoon, the contact team arrived.

More than just a single team. Twenty-one soldiers, led by a ground transport captain, made their way into Fox and summoned the town to the commons. By this time, the townspeople had received bits and pieces of what was happening. Over the last couple of hours, the Confederation had been attacking the Wolvic jamming, and there had been a few tiny gaps which allowed some information to be compressed and shot through. Things were not looking good, with San Isabella either fallen or close to it, joining other centers of gravity across the planet.

Les didn't understand how the Wolvics could hope to hold the entire planet, but that was what they seemed to be attempting. He didn't tell anyone else, but he figured that once some real combat forces arrived, the Wolvics would cede the field of battle and leave, their point made.

The captain was not able to give them much more information as to the status of the invasion, and Les suspected that the captain was just as much in the dark as he was. But he did collect Jack and the rest of the volunteers, sending them up with a staff sergeant to Listeville where transport would take them away to join the fight.

He didn't collect all of the volunteers. Some were turned down due to being under 18 or over 50. Winnie Hystad almost threw a fit when she wasn't allowed to join them. At 17 years old, she was a poolee, awaiting orders to boot camp in three months after her birthday. Les thought this was following regs a little too strictly. As soon as the Confederation Council placed Capernica under martial law, all of those restrictions would go out the window. But the captain was adamant, and seven of the sixty-four volunteers were turned back.

The fact that there were sixty-four volunteers warmed Les' heart. He'd never dreamed that so many would step forward. He felt a little guilty for doubting the patriotism of his fellow townspeople the evening before.

While the captain was speaking, Les sidled up to a master sergeant and introduced himself.

"Wade Koppleman," the soldier said, extending a hand. "We didn't have you on our list for Fox. Not that I'm surprised, I have to say. We do have a Commander dela Cort, though. Can you point him out?"

"He passed last year."

The master sergeant rolled his eyes. "Of course, he has. Why should our records be up-to-date? Well, we've got you here. I'll let the captain know. What was your MOS?"

"Mudhog. Like you."

"Hell, the first good news so far. Well, second. Our whole team almost ran into a fort this morning. The Wolvies had it right on our way, and we didn't have a clue."

"A Wolvie fort? No shit? What happened?"

"You're not going to believe this. Some boot louie took it out with a fucking civilian dozer. Smashed it to shit."

Les turned to look at him wondering if he was playing some sort of game with him. Wolvic forts were impressive strongpoints, needing combined arms to defeat. And a butterbar took it out with a bulldozer?

The guy looked serious, however. Les decided to let it ride for now and find out more later.

"So, you're a mudhog. What units?" Koppleman asked as if what he'd just said was an everyday occurrence.

"Retired from the Four-Twenty-Second. Medical," he said, smacking his hand against his knee. "Courtesy of pirates in the Avon Sector."

Koppleman hadn't noticed the hand before, but if it surprised him now, he didn't give any indication of that.

"Four-Twenty-Second? Pirates? You know Sergeant Major Ives? Didn't he get the Gold Nova there? He was my DI at Camp Reen."

Les laughed, earning a dirty look from the captain, who was droning on.

"Yeah, Private First Class Ives was in Charlie Company when he earned that. That was a long time ago," Les said, feeling old. "He made sergeant major? Where's he now?"

Les had always thought he'd make sergeant major, too, but his career had been cut short after losing his arm. Even now, not making sergeant major was one of his biggest regrets.

"Retired a couple of years ago. Went to Earth as a contractor, I heard."

If Les had felt old a moment ago, he felt even older now. PFC Ives had made sergeant major and retired, all since he'd arrived on Capernica?

"So, what's the scoop," he asked, wanting to change the subject. "Are we in Martial Law?"

"Fuck no. Waiting on the proclamation," he said in a whisper. "Word is that Council Prime's all wrapped up with Tanilite. Big Triple W push there."

"And we're just shit here?" Les said, not expecting an answer.

Triple W was one of the three governments on the other side of the war. They didn't have much in the way of ground forces, but their navy was top-of-the-line. Even with a big naval offensive, however, there should be ground troops to commit to Capernica.

"The Army's coming. In the meantime, we're supposed to gather up the volunteers and wait until we can start conscripting. Maybe tomorrow."

"We put up a few," Les said, nodding to where the Fox volunteers were getting ready to move out to Listeville.

"More across the river, in Little Fork and Brookstone."

Les raised his eyebrows in surprise. Brookstone was barely a bump along the River Road, and Little Fork, one of the earliest settlements on the planet, always seemed wrapped up in their own importance. Fox might be younger, but it had outgrown its cross-river rival.

Les knew he was probably being unfair, but most of the people on the river's west side considered themselves far superior in every way than the outnumbered Easterners.

"We've got to get over there and pick them up. All of the local volunteers will be gone tomorrow. Probably in the fight by morning, the poor bastards."

"Poor bastards is right. They'll be slaughtered," Les said.

"Along with most of the garrison," Koppleman said bitterly.

Les gave the master sergeant a sidewise glance. His face was red with anger. His fellow townspeople gathered around him and listening to the captain might think these 13 soldiers lucky, but Master Sergeant Koppleman burned with desire to be with the rest of his unit, even if that meant a probable death.

Les understood him like no civilian ever could.

"I can go pick up them up from across the river," Les said quietly.

"You've got a boat?" Koppleman asked, suddenly interested.

"No, but I can get one. A driver, too."

"Good shit, then. I'll let the captain know. One less thing to worry about. When can you go?"

Les looked over to where Emmeline was standing. As if she felt his gaze, she turned to look at him. She frowned as she took in the master sergeant standing next to him, and mouthed "what?"

He shook his head, then said, "Right now."

He wasn't about to ask his wife. Better to go do it now and explain later. He wasn't actually breaking any promises. It was just a short jaunt across the river and back. That's all.

He just hoped she'd see it the same way.

28

Chapter 4

Emmeline hadn't seen his jaunt across the river the day before in the same way as he did after all, not that he'd really expected her to. Still, no harm, no foul, and she'd let it go. She was watching him like a hawk, though, as he helped organize the town's defenses.

It wasn't as if anything they could do would have much effect against a concerted Wolvic attack. Fox was bounded by high hills on three sides and the river on the fourth. If the Wolvics wanted to level the town, all they had to do was sit on the high ground and pound it into submission. It wasn't as if they could do much to fortify the town itself—the ground was too rocky to do much digging. However, with the road the only overland way in and out, they could construct barricades along it that could theoretically slow down a Wolvic advance.

Theoretically.

As the only veteran in the town, more and more people were gravitating to him for advice, something that inflated his pride, but made Emmeline even warier. He tried to assure her that when the mayor asked him to honcho the building of the barriers, it didn't mean anything. It was just a precaution.

He knew Emmeline wasn't buying it. And for good reason. Given half a chance, he'd take off and join the fight. He didn't have that option only because even in an emergency, the Army didn't want old farts like him.

His back screamed out a complaint as he straightened from where he'd been kneeling to tack down one end of the wire, and as much as he didn't want to admit it, he knew why the Army didn't want him. His mind might still be sharp (sort of), but years in the infantry had taken a toll on his body, and not just to his right arm. Whoever engineered this entire aging thing needed to go back to the drawing board and come up with something different.

"Mr. Arceneaux, do you want more wire?" Winnie Hystad asked.

After being left behind the other volunteers due to her age, she'd lampreyed herself to Les as his assistant. He hadn't asked for the help, but he let it be. She was just trying to prove herself, something that he understood.

Besides, she was Juan dela Cort's granddaughter, and he owed his old friend this.

He looked over the barrier. It wouldn't stop any armor, but it could possibly tangle up trucks, and it would slow down infantry for a bit. Not good, but that wasn't its real purpose. The town needed to be proactive for their mental health. They had to be doing something. Another roll of wire wouldn't offer that much of an advantage, but it would give his crew of ten townspeople something more to do.

"Yeah, one more roll, if we've got it," he said.

"You heard him," she called out, pointing to Rail Singh. "Take the cart and fetch it."

Les had to suppress a smile. Rail Singh was a big man in his forties, a programmer for BTV. Twice Winnie's size and more than twice her age, he nevertheless just nodded and hopped on the cart to get the wire. Maybe the young woman had some potential. Juan would have been proud of her.

She caught him looking at her, then pointed past his shoulder. He turned to see Captain Parvel, Master Sergeant Koppelman, and the mayor trudging up the road to the barrier.

Captain Parvel was a little hard to read. Les had maybe 20 words with him in total since they arrived. He stood, hands on his hips, as he looked over the barrier, his face a blank slate. Les felt a little uncertain under that scrutiny.

"Better than I expected," Koppleman said. "It could buy you some time if it comes to that."

A very rough plan that was still being hashed out called for the townspeople to take to the water if the Wolvics advanced north on this side of the river. Les knew that would be a clusterfuck, so if the barrier could give them any more time at all, then this was not just an exercise in making everyone feel better. It could have a real benefit.

A couple of hardened MP90s would do a better job, but if he was wishing for the heavy automatic weapons stations, he might as well wish for a column of armor and a battalion of infantry in support. And air support, while he was at it.

"Any word on martial law?" he asked the master sergeant.

"Nothing firm. Comms are still intermittent. But it looks like maybe tomorrow morning local time."

Les felt a small wave of excitement wash over him. He couldn't volunteer due to his age, but under martial law and a conscription, he might not have a choice, and Emmeline couldn't blame him for that. It all depended on the parameters signed by the Council Prime.

"We need to be ready, so if you can arrange for four teams to get across the river, I'd appreciate it," Koppleman said.

Les raised an eyebrow. They only had seven teams in total, and sending four to the other side seemed excessive. There were more people on the west side of the river, and with San Isabella, this side should be the Wolvic's point of main effort.

"Sure, I can arrange that," he said before catching the mayor's glare.

Nyanne Morris took her mayoral duties seriously, and her position was a source of great pride to her. He realized that it had to gall her that the Army was going to him rather than her. Truth be told, there wasn't much in Fox for a mayor to do except hold meaningless meetings for those so inclined to attend. Les never did.

Still, he'd never had a problem with the mayor, and he'd just as soon keep it that way.

"With the mayor's OK, of course," he added.

"Of course, with the mayor's permission," Koppleman said as the captain turned around and started walking away, never having said a word.

The furrow in the mayor's brow lessened slightly as she turned and hurried after the captain.

"You won't need permission once martial law is declared," Les said.

"True that. But for now, best keep the local bosses happy," Koppleman said with a sigh. "I'd better go after them. Keep your powder dry."

"You, too," Les said, turning back to his working party.

Winnie was tearing apart some of the connectors, demanding that Jurgen and one of the newest residents, Wilma, Velma—something like that—take more care with them.

Yeah, Juan, I think your granddaughter's going to be a keeper.

Chapter 5

Master Sergeant Koppleman was correct. The martial law order broke through the jamming the next morning. The soldiers broke into a flurry of activity. Two teams headed north while four went down to the docks to get ferried across the river. Les went down to send them on their way.

"Are you sure you want to be left off at Grayson's?" Les asked. "That's a long way to hump to any of the towns on that side."

Grayson's was a high-end "rustic" resort along the Green River. The rustic was part of the design, hiding all of the high-tech amenities. Les had never been inside. A retired master sergeant's pay made the place more than a little out of reach for Emmeline and him.

"Eh, not a problem," Koppleman said quietly. "We've got a Class Mike depot there."

Les couldn't hide his surprise. Class Mike depots were scattered on most of the Confederation planets. Almost always unmanned, they kept a minimum of equipment and supplies prepositioned for emergencies, be the natural or manmade. Les just hadn't imagined that there would be one at Grayson's, and was surprised that he'd known nothing about it.

"Vehicles, weapons, that's where we need to be."

It was only then that Les noticed that the four teams were armed only with their personal weapons. The soldiers had arrived in Fox with several weapons mount-out boxes, but evidently, those weapons were only for the three teams remaining on this side of the river (the two teams going north and the one staying in Fox).

Slipping up, master sergeant, not noticing that.

"And speaking of which, we need to get going. I need to pick up my hover and drive up to Little Fork before noon. Got to welcome thirty-three new recruits into the Capernican Militia Self Defense Force, God help them," Koppleman said with a laugh as he patted his wristcomp. He turned to the river bus and yelled out, "Staff Sergeant Findley, we ready?"

Les stared at Koppleman's wristcomp, knowing that the names of the thirty-three were there.

"Uh, how many from Fox?" he asked.

"You already put out a good show, but the captain's got another fifty-two."

"And . . . uh . . . am I . . ." he started, unable to go ahead.

"Sorry, man. Too old," he said, putting an understanding hand on Les' shoulder. "I knew you'd want it, and I asked the captain to make an exception. You're twice the soldier any of these civilians are, but he's following the parameters."

"Hell, just as well. I'm too old for this shit," he said, his words at odds with his feelings.

"You take care of the town. Nice-looking place," Koppleman said, holding out his hand. "And thanks for your help."

Les took the hand, immediately feeling the small, hard object that the master sergeant transferred to his.

Ah, shit, and I don't have one to give him.

Master Sergeant Koppleman turned and stepped over the gunwale. As the bus pulled away, he looked back and gave Les a jaunty salute. Les waited until the bus was out in the current before he glanced at the challenge coin in his hand.

Gold, one side had the image of an eagle with 3051 Composite Squadron banner above, and the other side an image of Capernica. Les had a hundred challenge coins in his desk, but this was the first new one he'd received since he retired. He slipped it into his pocket and walked to the commons.

Martial law wasn't in effect for more than four more hours, but the captain was already passing the word. Les hadn't asked, but with the four teams crossing the river and two more already heading north, it looked like the captain would be leading the contact team to Fox. As he started to explain the conscription process, Les turned and walked back home. He already knew he wasn't on the list, but if he stayed for the reading of the names, he knew he would still stand there with bated breath, waiting to hear his name called out.

He stepped through the door to the unmistakable smell of jambalaya. That was proof that she was worried. In times of stress, she resorted to the foods of their youth on Pontchartrain. She turned at the sound of the door, relief flooding her face, and Les felt guilty for putting her through it all, especially as he wanted to go serve. If the Army would have taken him, he'd have jumped at the chance.

He silently walked up to her and pulled her to his chest in a hug. She gave a couple of shudders, then wrapped her arms around him, holding him tight. After a long moment, she pushed back, wiped the tears from her eyes, then said, "Sit."

She carried the pan over to the table and dished out the jambalaya for him, then for her. Les waited until she returned the pan, then sat down. Silently, the two crossed themselves, then began to eat.

Chapter 6

Early the next morning, he saw off the platoon as they marched uphill, past his barrier, to take a position on the high ground to the south of town. Most of the town was there, giving moral support, but with none of the celebration seen in the holovids when troops marched off to war.

Connectivity was much better now—still not perfect, but with the Confederation EES efforts breaking bigger holes in the Wolvic jamming. There wasn't much good news, and quite a bit bad.

Already, seven of the initial volunteers were dead, killed before they even made it to the fighting. The Wolvic air or drone forces had hit their truck shortly after leaving Listeville. One of them was John Woturu, who Les knew very well, having watched from next door as the boy grew into a man, got married, and had two children. Emmeline was cooking food at the moment to take over to Leah and the kids.

The seven wouldn't be the last of the losses, Les knew. He'd watched the conscripted townspeople drill the afternoon before, trying to help out, but while some turned out to be fair shots with the ancient Bradies they'd been issued, none of them understood how to act together as soldiers needed to be able to do. If the Wolvics came up in force, they'd be barely a speed bump on the road.

Captain Parvel evidently knew that, too. With the fifty-five townspeople and three soldiers, he could have broken the unit into two platoons, but with his two soldiers being a corporal and a PFC, he didn't have a second platoon commander, and he kept them all in one oversized platoon. Les knew he had the experience to take a platoon, and he'd offered his services, but his name was not on the list generated by some AI located deep in the bowels of Army Headquarters half a galaxy away, so to the captain, that was not an option.

He didn't think he needed to tell Emmeline that he'd volunteered.

At least the captain had some tactical sense. Les had been concerned. Being infantry, he had a typically low opinion of the fighting ability of POGs. They could be great at their jobs and were needed for the Army to function, but it took combat arms soldiers to take the fight to the enemy. But the captain understood that he could do no good in the town itself. Fox would become a shooting gallery in a fight.

By moving to the high ground to the south, he'd accomplish two things. First, he'd remove any reason for Fox to become a Wolvic target. The Wolvics were signatories of the Accords, which required that civilians who were not offering resistance could not be targeted. Second, he was giving his platoon a fighting chance to inflict damage on the invaders.

Winnie Hystad paced the platoon, head close to Lane Porter-Manuel. Lane was a classmate of Winnie's, and he'd been conscripted. Winnie, to her chagrin, had not, and she'd given the captain an earful. But just as Les had been unsuccessful in getting the man to change the orders, so had she.

Winnie stopped at the barrier, which had been opened to let the platoon through, and as the last of them passed, took over to close the barrier back up.

"Les, we've got a meeting at Leon's," Nyanne said as the platoon marched around the bend in the road as they climbed.

"About what?" Les asked, watching them disappear.

"About what? About the damned invasion, and what we're going to do about it. You're our only expert left."

The fighting was bypassing those of them left in the village, and Les had no desire to sit in a meeting that would undoubtedly go on for hours, accomplishing nothing. All he wanted to do was go home and take a nap.

Still, duty was duty, and even if he couldn't get in the fight, he knew he had something to offer.

"I'll be right there," he said, as the last rank disappeared from sight.

Chapter 7

Les' wristcomp vibrated with another message just as they pulled the hulk of Ron Steven's old water taxi to the dock. He heaved back on the line, struggling to pull it over the bollard, when something popped, and he dropped to his knees in pain.

His entire body ached after two days of work, but he was afraid he'd done some actual damage this time. He lay down on his back, staring at the sky, when Winnie's "Oh, shit," caught his attention.

At first, he'd been more bemused by Winnie's attention than anything else, but she'd proven herself to be a godsend, an indefatigable font of energy. He'd come to rely more and more on her as his right hand while preparing the town for any number of potential possibilities.

He twisted his neck to where she was up by the bow, staring at her wristcomp.

What now? We lost another city?

Connectivity was slowly getting better, but only for official notices. The commercial undernet was either shut down or unable to get past the jamming, but the government was able to send burst transmissions that got through. Les didn't know how much to trust what was being passed, and he had a feeling that things were worse in reality.

He opened the messaging, read the headline, and the gut punch made him forget all about his back. He swung over onto his stomach and linked to the story.

"Oh, shit" was an understatement. The Wolvic advance on the east side of the river had razed Brookstone. Not just taken it, but burned it to the ground. There were massive civilian casualties.

Les' first thought was that it was BS. He'd served alongside the Wolvics back when they were allies, and they hadn't struck him as evil people. Politics and allegiances may have changed over the years, but he couldn't imagine why the

Capernican or Confederation leaders would lie about that. He had to take the report at face value.

But why? Then he remembered several instances of "excesses," as the command referred to them, over his 26 years of service. Sometimes, things get out-of-hand, despite the best of intentions. But a whole town? More than a thousand people?

He stumbled to his feet, pain shooting from his back to his toes. "Take care of this thing, Winnie. Remember, all it has to do is float. It's going to get towed."

"Got it," Winnie said.

He could hear her taking over as he left the dock, taking care to keep his back straight. He cursed his aging body and just hoped he hadn't done any serious damage.

Les wasn't the only one heading for Ryan's. There were at least 40 people inside as he pushed through the door, and Nyanne was calling for quiet. Rock Goring put his fingers in his mouth and gave a piercing whistle that threatened eardrums, and the place quieted down.

"Thank you, Rock," the mayor said. "I know you all got the message. I . . . I'm at a loss for words. Brookstone. I can't believe it. Before we start, has anyone checked on Bess and Loudon?"

Les winced. Bess and Loudon's son had just taken his family and relocated to Brookstone. If the report was accurate about the massacre . . .

He didn't want to dwell on that right not.

"Tantan is on her way. I saw her on the way here," someone in front said.

"Can we get someone else to help her with them? Bobbie? Maybe you?"

Bobbie White Bear was a carpenter, but he was also the founder and lay minister for Hope Chapel, the town's nondenominational church. He was heavily involved with town politics, and Les knew he wanted to be part of this meeting, but he nodded and went to tend to Bess and Loudon.

"OK, as you all heard, Brookstone's been attacked."

"They kilt them all, Nyanne. They didn't just attack," Massie Winston shouted out. "Just like they're gonna do here."

"We don't know that," the mayor said. "We don't even know for sure if there's anyone coming our way."

"Where else are they going to go?" Rock asked.

Frankly, Les was surprised they'd crossed the river at San Isabella instead of heading up north on this side of the river first. But Rock had a point. Other forces had landed on the mainland, and even here on Grande Isle, another force had taken the southern port of Crystal Bay. After yesterday's battle on the Plains of David, there weren't that many more places with any significant populations. The Wolvics in the province could consolidate and marry up with their forces on the mainland, but the transit could leave them vulnerable if the Army and the Navy arrived while they were moving.

"What do we do when they come? Declare this a free town? Run away? Fight?" Indigo al Gova asked. Indigo was one of Fox's founding residents, and his opinion carried a lot of weight among the others. Leave it to him to get to the crux of the matter.

Declaring a free town would be ceding it to the Wolvics, and they'd be placing the citizens at their mercy. This might save the people and homes, but when the Army eventually came, that declaration still held. The Confederation Army would have to take it back while the townspeople huddled and tried to stay alive in the fight.

Fleeing would get the townspeople out of harm's way, but where would they go? Downriver would be out, and upriver would only be delaying the inevitable. Crossing would put them at risk from the Wolvics advancing up that side. Lives were more important than property, but if the Wolvics found an empty town, they'd raze it to the ground.

Fighting wouldn't delay the Wolvics by much, but if they declared their intention to fight, the Wolvics would be forced to treat the survivors as POWs. If there were survivors. But the decision might have already been taken out of their hands.

"We've already decided," Les said, speaking up. "Captain Parvel and our young men and women are up in the pass right now, preparing for a fight. From the Wolvie's perspective, that means we're fighting."

There was a mass of protests, all too jumbled to make any sense. The mayor shouted for quiet, but to no avail.

Les already knew the outcome. They'd keep making plans to flee upriver, hoping to keep ahead of the Wolvics until the Army arrived. He just hoped that Captain Parvel and his oversized platoon would give them the time they needed to get everyone out of the town when the time came.

It would take them several hours to realize the inevitability of that, several hours that he could put to use getting as many boats and hulls ready as possible. He pushed his way through those still arriving and limped back to the town docks.

Chapter 8

"This is . . . impressive," the mayor said as she stood with Les, looking at the small navy of boats, hulls, and rafts jamming the riverfront. "I didn't know we had this much here in town."

Neither did I.

For the first 36 years of Fox's existence, the only way in and out was on the river. The first dirt road eased the burden, and when the road was paved, more and more traffic went overland. Older boats, no longer necessary, were pulled ashore and stashed wherever they could.

Les had every mechanic he could scare up working on engines or hulls, but some of the craft would never get underway under their own power. They'd have to be towed. But if Bennie Ricapito, an old river pilot, was right, then they'd just about have enough spaces to get everyone who was left out of Fox. Of course, it helped that over a hundred had volunteered or were conscripted to fight, and another two hundred or so had already left for towns farther north or had hiked into the mountains to hide out.

Les didn't know to where the flotilla would go—just that it would be upriver—and he knew that if it did put to the water, they'd be sitting ducks for any Wolvic attack. That was beyond the scope of his present duties, however. He had to trust the mayor and town council to consider all of that.

The mayor stepped down the bank, put her hands on the gunnels of a hull, and looked inside. "Is this thing going to float? There's a hole in it."

"It'll be fixed. Julie and Lars have it on their list," he said, pointing to where the two were patching up another hull.

The mayor started to walk over to them when a series of dull booms resonated from up the grade. She stopped, a confused look on her face, but Les' heart sunk into his gut. He'd recognized the sounds of war, and he'd been half-expecting something would happen to Captain Parvel's small force, hoping that it wouldn't.

Les bolted away from the docks, ignoring the mayor's questions that chased him. His house was on Robin Street, just two blocks from the river. Cutting through yards and vaulting fences, he was home in less than a minute.

He powered up his Ion, glad that Emmeline was making the rounds of those households that had already lost family. He didn't need that confrontation now.

His dash flashed green, and he was about to pull out when he hesitated, looking in through his front window to his I Love Me wall. He felt naked, going to find out what he was sure had happened, but hoped desperately had not.

No, I've already thought of this. You can't look like a threat until you know what you're facing.

He pulled out onto the road and started gunning it to Adams when a shape ran in front of him. His nerves heightened, instinct almost took over, and he sped up before he recognized Winnie waving her arms at him to halt. He skidded to a stop, almost sideswiping her, and looked back to the docks, afraid for a moment that the Wolvics had landed by the river.

"What is it?" he shouted, righting the bike to go around her.

Before he quite knew what was happening, she slid by him and jumped on the back of the bike, arms clamped around his waist.

"I'm going with you."

Anger flared for a second, and he started to protest, but he damped it down. It was her choice. And, he was ashamed to admit, it might be safer with a couple, just a man and woman trying to find safety.

He spun the bike onto Adams, then to the San Isabella Highway. People were coming out of buildings, looking up the grade, where smoke and dust were rising into the sky.

There was something else up there, too, something the others would have missed. Les knew what he was looking for, however. It was just a ripple high on Kirsten Peak, in front of a rock face, as if he was looking through a heat wave rising off the road. Another ripple briefly flickered, then disappeared.

"Shit," he muttered as he drove around the barrier and started up the grade.

He knew the moment it happened that the town's militia unit had been hit and hit hard. It could have been hit by aircraft or even an orbital platform, just a target of opportunity. Or, more threatening, it could have just had fire called upon it by a disc-recon team.

Those two flickers gave him the answer. The militia platoon had been targeted, and that meant the town was in the way of a Wolvic advance.

Wolvics loved their discs, floating circles that could carry a soldier and equipment over 200 klicks before getting a new fuel cell. The straight leg infantry liked to use them in plain sight to cow their enemies, something Les thought was stupid. Their disc-recon, however, could range far and wide, over any terrain, quickly and easily. With high-speed, low-drag cloakers, they were essentially invisible—unless an opposing soldier knew what to look for.

Les did.

The recon team had called for the fire on the platoon, and they also had a direct line-of-sight on Fox below them. He was lucky to see their movement, probably shifting slightly to check the reaction from the town. Disc-recon would not just call for fire on a Capernican militia platoon unless there was a reason. As per their SOP, they tended to husband their resources. The most probable reason they targeted the platoon was that there was a Wolvic advance coming up the highway. The team would now be providing fire support for the oncoming unit.

Les almost stopped and returned. They'd have noted the two of them, after all, and disc-recon were all sniper qualified. But he had to see what had happened. There could be wounded soldiers up there, people he knew. Almost the instant he considered turning around, he rejected the idea.

Going to investigate what happened would be a normal reaction, so he hoped the disc-recon would let them be, not wanting to give up their position.

Still, he could almost feel the crosshairs of a sniper scope on his chest as they climbed the grade. If the team wanted to take them out, there was no use making it easy for them, so he pushed the switchbacks hard. Too hard, really, but the big bike's tires bit into the road, keeping them steady.

For the first time, he really noticed Winnie behind him, her grip tightening each time they whipped around a curve. He now regretted not kicking her off the bike. He was putting her into too much danger, about which she was clueless.

They crested the pass, smoke and dust still rising ahead of them. Captain Parvel had chosen Thule Meadow to make his stand, a hectare or so of relatively flat land where Kyoma Creek flowed over a waterfall and down to Green River. It wasn't a bad choice. He could dig in his troops to an extent, and it was in defilade to anyone coming up the highway.

The two rode around the last curve leading to it and into hell. The trees and bushes were flattened into kindling, and the creek itself was a muddy marsh. Several prone trees had flames licking at them.

Les recognized the pattern. A salvo of B-rounds, which provided overpressure that flattened buildings and trees—and unprotected troops—followed by HD-rounds that riddled the area with shrapnel. Mech troops might survive such a salvo, but unprotected infantry . . .

Winnie slid off the back of the bike, running into the kill zone, screaming out names. Les would help her in a moment, but he had to figure out how Wolvic artillery had managed to hit the meadow. This wasn't air, nor missiles, and the high ground to the south should have meant artillery couldn't reach it—one reason why Captain Parvel had chosen the location.

As he looked to his left, it became clear. The Thule Meadow did not look down upon the San Isabella Highway, but it did look down on the other side of the river, and for quite a way south. The disc-recon had called for fire from artillery on the other side of the river.

Les wanted to kick himself. He should have realized that would be possible and warned the Captain. If the disc-recon team could see the meadow . . .

Slowly, Les turned around, keeping his head level as if he was looking at the carnage. His eyes, however, angled up. The immediate hills around the meadow gave good protection from the higher ground with one exception. Right over the flattened trees, over the bare rock, a section of the mountain was visible, right about where he'd seen the ripples. With a sightline to the meadow and another to the town, he knew this was where the team was.

Les pushed the bike as close to the edge of the meadow as he could, using the nearest hill to keep him just out of sight from the disc-recon's hide. Then he joined Winnie to search for survivors. He knew the chances of any of them still being alive was minimal, but he had to make sure.

Winnie was ashen as she ran from position to position, but she was still functional. That was saying something. The B-round imploded bodies, leaving a mass of jelly where once living, breathing humans had been. The HE rounds then tore up what was left. Years of experience had taught Les to compartmentalize the deaths, to make them simply part of the landscape, no different from a dead rabbit at the side of the road. He'd mourn later, when the shakes started, but he didn't have time for that now.

After five minutes, he caught Winnie and told her, "That's enough. No one survived."

"But maybe—" she started, her voice cracking.

"We've checked everyone."

"I . . . what do we do now?" she said, choking on the words.

"We go back to Fox."

"But what about them. Shouldn't we do something?"

"We can't on my bike. We'll go down to Fox, and when all this is over, we'll take care of them."

"I saw Renee," she said quietly. "I recognized her shoes. The rest of her . . ."

Les had often seen Winnie and Renee running wild about the town. They must have been close.

"I can't have you break down on me now, Winnie. I need you to hold it together. OK?"

She took a long look around the meadow, took five deep breaths, and seemed to gather herself. "What do you want me to do?"

"Get back to my bike and wait for me."

"What are you going to do?"

"I'll be there in a second. Just go."

She nodded and walked off, her body stiff. Les followed, never looking up, but watching for the moment he'd be masked again from the disc-recon's hide.

As soon as he was, he quickly looked at what was left of the few positions on this side of the meadow. He pounced on a Bamberger lying on the ground, one of the contact team's, but it was mangled beyond use.

Shit, I could have used that.

Under another jellied body, he saw a barrel. It was a Brady—an underpowered piece of shit, but still a military weapon. He shook off some of the blood and tissue and worked the action. Part of the stock was broken, but it looked like it was functional.

He spent another minute looking, but didn't find anything else salvageable. He was hoping for more, but at least it was something.

Les returned to the bike where Winnie was watching him. She grimaced at the blood-covered rifle but didn't say anything. He slid the weapon under the seat straps on the right side of the bike, where the bike's body and the two of them should be able to hide it from the disc-recon team's view.

The team probably still wanted to maintain their secrecy, hopefully thinking that there was no one in the town who knew what to look for. It was a reasonable assumption. Anyone with army military experience would probably be joining the fight. They might not have considered that there were old farts like him.

If they wanted to maintain their secrecy, then they might let the two of them go. If the team saw them carrying weapons, however, that might change, and taking them out almost anywhere on the grade should be child's play to them.

"Can you drive this thing?" he asked Winnie.

"I don't know. Probably," she said, eyeing the bike. "Why?"

"Because there's a Wolvie team up there that might decide to take us out. If they do, and get me, I want you to gun this sucker and get down the hill. Tell the mayor that the Wolvies are coming, and they need to evacuate the city."

She spun around, as if she could spot the team.

"They can't see us right here. But when we're on the road, they can, so act normal. Don't look up to try and spot them."

"I . . . OK. I can do that. But, if you, I mean, if they shoot, they'll hit me, not you, so you can keep going, right?"

"You're driving. I'm riding shotgun."

"But—"

"But nothing. You're smaller than me. Their round would probably get both of us with you in back."

Which was possibly true, but the fact of the matter was that Les was feeling guilty for bringing her. She had too much of her life ahead of her. She'd be a good sailor someday, but she had to survive the war.

"Why don't you drive and just go balls to the wall?" she asked.

"Because that would probably spark them to shoot. Like a cat who sees something scurrying away."

"Like a cat?" she asked as if he was crazy.

"Hey, it was the best I could come up with." He motioned her to get on the bike. "We can't keep them wondering what we're doing. We need to go now."

She tentatively got on, her legs barely reaching the pegs. He got on behind her. Reaching around her, he put the bike on autocommand, something no true biker would ever do.

"Throttle and break. That's all you need to remember. The bike will do the rest."

As lanky as he was, he could reach around her to both controls, and taking her hands, he placed them, then edged the bike forward. She applied a bit too much throttle, but on autocommand, the bike compensated. They slowly road over the pummeled ground before they reached the highway. Les dropped his hands from the throttle and grabbed her around the waist as they turned north and climbed to the pass.

If Les had felt the sniper's crosshairs on him before, it was intensified now. He'd never even hear the shot fired. In an instant, the hypervelocity dart would pierce his back, the fins deploying to make mincemeat of his internal organs.

He tried not to think of that as they crested the pass and started down the grade. With Fox in view, it would suck big time to be cut down now.

"There they are!" someone shouted as they reached the bottom. People started to swarm them, shouting out questions.

"Do I stop?" Winnie asked.

"Tell the mayor to start the evacuation now!" Les yelled as he reached around her and took off across the primary school lawn, darting around the people pushing forward to them.

The bike didn't have its normal oomph on autocommand, but it was still an Ion-6, and he easily outpaced the group and made it past them, cutting through the playground and onto Adams. A few moments later, he pulled in front of his house and cut the motor.

"What do we do now?" Winnie asked as they got off the bike.

"We're going hunting."

Chapter 9

Les pulled the Brady free of the Ion's straps. "Clean this up, will you?"

Winnie's eyes barely flickered as he handed her the bloody weapon.

Good. She's controlling her emotions.

"You're not going to leave me here, are you?" she demanded.

"I haven't decided yet. Just be back here in fifteen minutes," he said before turning and heading for the door.

"I'm going with you," Winnie shouted at his back. "Don't you forget that!"

Les slipped inside his front door and locked it. He didn't want to be interrupted. The smell of gumbo permeated the house from the pot on the stove, and his stomach growled. He ignored it.

First things first, he told himself as he walked into the single bedroom he shared with Emmeline. He opened the closet and pulled out a battered footlocker. Inside were the remnants from his time in service. He hadn't seen them in years, but he knew every item in it. On top was his neatly folded alphas, medals hanging from the chest. He'd last worn it at his retirement ceremony. He took a moment to stroke the Purple Heart and Order of the Gryphon as memories threatened to overwhelm him, then pushed the blouse aside. Now wasn't the time for that.

Underneath the alphas were his field fatigues. The smart fabric had long lost its charge, so they were a dull tannish-green, but the lack of camouflage didn't matter. Not for his purposes. He shucked his shirt and jeans, then pulled on his fatigues. Despite the years, they were like welcoming an old friend. They felt right.

And they still fit, he thought, with more than a little pride.

He couldn't help but step into the bathroom and look into the mirror. He was bald, his beard gray, and wrinkles now creased his face, but if he squinted hard enough, he could almost see that gung-ho PFC getting ready for his first taste of combat.

He was well aware that this could be—*probably* would be—his last taste, one way or the other. At least now, with his uniform on, he was a combatant. As a soldier, even a retired soldier, carrying a weapon out of uniform could classify him as a spy, unprotected by the Accords. Not that it really mattered much, in the grand scheme of things. But if this was going to be his last hoorah, he wanted to go out in full compliance with the regulations. Regulations are made the difference between a mob and an army, and he had his pride. He was a soldier.

Les pulled down on the bottom of his blouse to straighten it, gave himself one last look-over, then headed to the small desk in the corner of the room. He'd scrounged it upon arriving in Fox, and it had become the handy receptacle for papers, books, underwear, or anything else that he was too lazy to put in its place. He didn't care about all of that now, however. Les pulled open the drawer and rummaged around, pushing detritus of the last couple of decades around. He grabbed an old medical kit and snapped it to his belt, then kept looking for his main objective. It wasn't there. Panic started to set in, and he pulled the drawer out, upending it on the floor before kneeling and frantically searching.

And there it was. His fingers closed around the small module in relief.

Back in the 20th and 21st Centuries on Earth, there was an organization for young boys and girls whose motto was "Be prepared." Les had embraced that motto, letting it guide him through his military career. Even after retiring and moving to Fox. Now, that preparation was going to pay off.

The module was highly illegal to be in his possession. If it had ever been discovered, he'd do jail time and probably lose his pension. But he had it, and that was all that mattered.

"Thanks, Gemi," he said as he left the bedroom for the living room and his I Love Me wall. He stood there a moment before he reached up and unhooked his old ME2 MEW from its cradle.

If putting on his fatigues was like welcoming an old friend, holding the MEW was like embracing a lover. A wave of emotions swept through him. The two of them had gone through so much together.

But the MEW was dead, not the lover of his memory. His organic hand almost caressed the weapon as he slid it to the chamber access and flipped it open. With muscle memory that hadn't faded over the years, he slipped in the syn-module, feeling it click into place. The MEW came alive as energy pulsed through it.

"Now, that's my girl. That's more like it."

LEDs flashed along the barrel as it powered up, and within 20 seconds, the weapon hummed with deadly intention. Les took a quick glance at the power readout: 82 percent.

"Not bad after all this time."

The power pack had been quiescent all this time, just waiting for the syn-module to power up the weapon. Les had been more than half-afraid the MEW would remain dead, but it was running through the start-up as if was brand new. Less than a minute after he inserted the module, it was combat-ready.

He brought the weapon to his shoulder. For most of his career, Les was righthanded. A young pirate, not much more than a girl, had changed that when she took his arm. Now, he was left-handed, and bringing the MEW up to his left shoulder felt a little awkward. Still, he felt much more confident than he'd been when he'd returned into the house.

The ME2 MEW was a heavy, powerful weapon, part of a trend to energy rifles that dominated the armories when he'd enlisted. Throwing out gigajoules in focused meson beams, they could boil any organic tissues and take out armor and were feared by infantry . . . until modern armor was developed to defeat it. And the armor was pretty simple, most easily understood as reflective armor that simply bounced the beams aside. A beast to lug around, power-hungry, and with long recycle times, they were slowly replaced with the still current trend to hypervelocity darts which could easily pierce the old reflective armor.

The beamers were gradually replaced with the new generation of weapons, and without the threat, the heavy reflective armor, at least for infantry, became obsolete.

With the beamers being retired, Les was able to keep his—without the module, of course. Except that his buddy, Chief Warrant Officer Four Gemi Johannes, the battalion armorer, had managed, through physical and bureaucratic sleight-of-hand, to slip him a module.

Be prepared.

The door opened, and Les turned to see Emmeline come through. She looked up at him, and he could almost see her body deflate.

"Em . . ."

"I knew it. I always knew that damned thing wasn't deactivated. You lied to me."

"It was. I mean . . . the module . . ."

"And now you're going to get yourself killed, right? The knight riding off to defeat the dragon."

"I—"

"Don't," she snapped. "Don't even try to justify yourself." A tear glistened in her eye, and she quietly asked, "Don't you think you've done enough?"

He stood there, three meters and a hundred klicks apart. He wanted to take her in his arms, swear that things would be all right. But he couldn't. He couldn't lie to her.

The door opened, and the mayor stuck her head in the room.

"What the hell's going on, Les," she asked. "I got your message, then I saw Em go inside. What happened up there. Are our people OK?"

"No."

"How many?" she asked, one hand drifting to her chest.

"All of them."

She took a step back, looked around, then came inside, shutting the door.

"Are you sure? All of them?" she asked, her voice breaking.

"I'm sure. And I'm sure the Wolvies are coming. Soon. You've got to get the people out of here."

The mayor looked at the floor for a long moment, then asked, "How long do we have?"

"I really don't know. An hour. Half a day. How ever long it is, you can be sure it isn't enough. You need to move now."

She seemed only then to realize that he was in his fatigues and was armed. "What about you?"

"We've got a disc-recon team with eyes on the town. They can call fire on all of you, so I'm going to see what I can do about that."

Emmeline gasped, and Nyanne stared hard at him before nodding. Les could see the mayor in her take charge.

"Good luck, and I hope we see you again when all of this is over," she said before turning away.

She doesn't think I'll make it. Well, neither do I.

He was glad that she didn't try and change his mind. There was no time for fake theatrics.

"Les, answer me this. Do you really need to do this?" Emmeline asked as she stepped forward and put her arms around his back.

"If they wait until everyone is loading, they can take the entire town out with a couple of rounds. You weren't up there at Thule Meadows. They didn't have a chance."

She hugged him tighter, and he could feel the hot tears soak through his blouse. A couple of days ago, the tears were in relief. Now they were for a far darker reason.

"I don't suppose you have time to eat. I made gumbo. It might be ready."

"Two times in one week. You're going to spoil me, like a true cajun woman." He gently disengaged her arms, then kissed her on the head. "But no, I don't have time."

She lunged at him, arms around his neck in a death grip, and kissed him with a passion he barely remembered.

"You better come back, Boo. I'll kick your ass if you don't," she said when they came up for air.

"Yes, ma'am!"

She gave him one last long look, then turned to the entryway, taking him by the hand.

"Are you going alone?" she asked as they reached the door.

"No, I'm taking the Hystad girl. Winnie." He hadn't realized he'd already made up his mind about that until just then.

"But she's just a kid."

"She's seventeen, and she's already enlisted." He held his hand up, palm out to cut off her protests. "Besides, I've seen a lot of her over these past days. I trust her with my back."

He opened the door, and Winnie was already there leaning up against his Ion, the Brady clean.

"Get down to the docks now, Em. Tell Lars I want you on the Gracie May."

He might as well get something out of all of this, and the Gracie May was a hover river bus with a much higher speed than any of the prop-boats. He gave her a kiss, then a gentle push on the butt in the direction of the docks.

"I'll be down there soon enough."

Winnie watched him apprehensively as he approached, waiting for his decision.

"Can you fire that thing?" he asked as he swung his leg over the seat.

"Better than you, Mr. Arceneaux," she said, a smile breaking out over her face.

"In your dreams. And since you're coming, how about we drop the Mr. Arceneaux crap. Sergeant. Or Les. Your choice."

"Sergeant," she said as she got on behind him.

He pulled out an armband from his pocket and handed it to her. "Make sure you wear this. It's your uniform."

"Mr. Arceneaux," another voice called before he could pull out.

Miklos Nagy was running up to him, his baby son bouncing in one arm, an old shotgun in the other.

Les couldn't spare the time, but he owed this to the young man.

"Up there, did you find . . . did you see Suki?" he choked out as he entered the yard.

"I'm sorry, son. I saw her," he said, shaking his head.

"She's . . . she's gone?"

Les nodded.

Emmeline crossed over to him and took little Kris, and put an arm around the young man. She'd had years of practice consoling the spouses of lost soldiers.

Miklos didn't break down, however. He stared at Les with an intensity that made him sit back farther on his bike.

"You're going back, aren't you? You're going after the bastards who killed her," he said, his voice hard as steel, cold as ice.

Les nodded.

"Where are they?"

Les said, "Up there, on the face, where the rocks show white."

Miklos looked up there, hate pouring from him. "I'm coming with you."

That was it. No asking. No discussion. He was just stating a fact.

"No, you're not. You've got Kris to take care of."

"I'm not asking you. I'm going. If you won't take me, I'll go on my own. But I bet you don't know about the Heaven trail. Right?"

Les had heard about the infamous Heaven trail, of course. But he and Emmeline had come to Fox long after they needed to sneak off on lovers' trysts. All he knew was that there was a trail up there somewhere.

He turned to look at Winnie, who blushed and admitted, "I never went up. No reason to, you know."

"I can get you pretty close to that. We can take the bike part way, but the rest is a good long hike."

"Your son," Emmeline said. "He needs you."

"He needed Suki more."

"He's got no one."

"I'm a pretty shitty father. I know you all think I'm a drunk. Well, I am. Suki's parents are down in Belfast City. He'll do much better with them."

Les' heart went out to him, but the boy was acting in the heat of the moment. He needed to calm down.

"Stay with your son," he said.

Miklos frowned and shook his head. He leaned over and kissed Kris on the top of his sandy-haired head.

"Get him to Suki's parents when this is all done," he told Emmeline, then abruptly turned and started jogging over to Adams, going against the flow of people heading to the docks.

Les gave Emmeline a beseeching look, wondering what to do. She hugged little Kris closer and said, "Take him with you. He's got a better chance to make it through with you than alone."

Les mouthed, "I love you," as he gunned the Ion, catching up to Miklos in ten seconds.

"Get on," he said, tossing him his old fatigue cap. "You're taking us up Heaven Trail."

Chapter 10

"I think this is as far as we can go," Les said, stopping the bike. "How long from here, do you think?"

Miklos looked up the mountain. "We're not far. Maybe forty minutes?"

Les looked back down toward the town. He couldn't see it from this spot, but the last time it was in view, five minutes ago, there wasn't as much progress as he'd hoped. It had only been about half an hour since he'd told the mayor to evacuate, but even dealing with civilians, surely more would have been ready. Almost all of the boats within his view were still there.

At least they'd made good time, and it was fortunate they had Miklos as a guide. He'd have missed the trail, choosing one of the others which would not have gotten them that far or even could have been exposed to the Wolvics. The trail to Heaven was out of view of the disc-recon team and was narrow, but clear. Even beyond the spot where young lovers did what young lovers do, he'd been able to climb another couple hundred meters before the bike just couldn't go any farther.

The three got off the Ion and started up on foot. Miklos wanted to lead, but the kid's shotgun didn't have the range of his MEW, and Winnie's Brady didn't have the punch.

Les started with a pretty aggressive pace, and within a minute or two, his legs started protesting. He muttered a curse under his breath. Back in the day, the hill would be nothing, but now . . .

There was nothing to do but push on. He could rest when he was dead.

But his body just couldn't take a sprint up the mountain. He had to stop twice, lungs bellowing for air. Both times he'd held up a hand for silence, then cocked his head as if listening for the enemy. Juvenile, yes, but he couldn't help it.

Miklos said the trail went all the way to the peak where the adventurous overnighted to watch the sunrise. Les was just glad they weren't going that far. Gray spots were floating across his eyes when Miklos grabbed his shoulder and said they'd gone far enough. The Wolvics should be at about this elevation.

Les bent over, hands on his knees, ignoring his pride. He had to catch his breath before continuing. Miklos moved past him and stood there protectively, shotgun at the ready.

"Are you OK?" Winnie asked in a whisper.

"Yeah. Just give me a moment," Les wheezed out.

It had been so easy to decide to attack the Wolvics on the mountain when he was back in Fox. It was easy to insist that he was still combat-ready. The reality of old age was kicking him hard in the ass now, however.

It took two long minutes before he could go on. He refused to look Miklos in the eye as he pushed past him.

Ahead, he could see the side of the rock face, rising another 250 meters before it flattened out somewhat and led to the peak. Somewhere up there, around on the other side, the Wolvic disc-recon team should be.

Hopefully.

The team could have displaced, he knew. They had discs, so they could have flown up to a crag or depression in the rock face, giving them a better view and taking them out-of-range of Miklos' shotgun for sure, maybe even his MEW.

Watching the holovids, it would be easy to assume that energy weapons, even fictional "ray guns," had unlimited ranges. In the vacuum of space, that was essentially true. In an atmosphere, however, the effective range dissipated quickly due to sublimation, heat generation, and several more "tions," especially on a planet like Capernica with its denser atmosphere. Tanks, beam artillery, and aircraft could amp up the power output to counteract those degrading factors, but mudhogs had to carry their powerpacks, and they had to be small enough to insert into their weapons. Firing his MEW,

Les could shoot at someone across the river, and while they could see the blast, meaning the beam reached them, it wouldn't do much more than make their eyes itch.

Compounding the issue, within their cloaking bubbles, Les wouldn't be able to aim directly on his targets. He'd have to use the second broadest beam to ensure he hit the soldier within the bubble. Taking that into account, to drop someone in the light armor recon-types preferred, he'd have to be within 250 meters or so. 150 was even better for an immediate kill. The MEW could kill from much farther out, but the dying would take time, time where the target could bite back.

There was no use worrying about it until he could figure out the situation, and that would take more time than he wanted. Footing was treacherous scrambling over the scree, and a misplaced step could send them tumbling.

They managed to get to the edge of the rock face in one piece. Les told the other two to get down, then he crept on his belly to get a better view. The rock stretched up, almost vertically. At the base, scree and dirt, with a few interspersed scraggly trees, were fairly level for ten or twenty meters before the ground sloped down to the trees below. Les tried to think back to the flickers he'd seen from the town and place that up here like an overlay. They had to be near the base, he realized. At the moment, he had a good view of Fox, but much lower, and the trees would block the view. Once again, though, they had discs. They could pop up as needed.

No, they wanted to conserve energy. The discs would be powered down, the powerpack just energizing the cloaking. When soldiers were isolated from the supply lines, they tended to hoard food, water, energy, and ordnance. They'd probably been doing that since Phoenician times.

So, where are you?

Counterintuitively, the closer a soldier was to a cloaked target, the harder it was to discern. Les relied on an old mudhog trick. He looked down the slope, not directly at the base of the rock face, relaxing his eyes. It took a few minutes, but it paid off. His peripheral vision caught the ripples.

Got you!

It wasn't good, but it could be worse. The two were halfway across the base of rock face, maybe 250 meters away. With the cloaking engaged, he couldn't make anything out. Cloaking alone provided no protection, though, and if he could get close enough, he was sure his MEW would do the job.

There was no cover, however, between his spot and the Wolvic team. They'd have to cross open ground before the Wolvics knew they were there.

Beyond them, a low rumble sounded in the distance. The rumble of war. The main advance was underway. No, maybe not the main advance, or at least the only one, he realized. From his vantage spot, smoke rose across the river to the south.

Hell, they've got a two-pronged advance, paralleling the river.

Not that that changed anything for them. He wished the Easterners well, but he had to take this team out so the townspeople could make their escape.

If the Wolvics are coming up the highway, I bet the team is watching them. Maybe they'll be a little complacent about their rear.

It was a huge assumption, but at this point, Les was grasping at straws.

He backed up to where Winnie and Miklos were anxiously waiting.

"Did you spot them?" Miklos asked.

"Yeah. They're at the base of the rock face, about two-hundred-and-fifty meters away."

"You said you wanted less than two hundred," Winnie said, stroking the stock of her Brady. "But this will reach them."

"I can't see them through the cloaking. I don't know how they're outfitted with armor. If we had a Bamberger, I'd risk it, but if we use that toy, all it'll do is let them know we're here."

"But they'll know we're here as soon as we move. It's all open at the base of the face," Miklos said.

Les had forgotten that Miklos had been all over the mountain growing up. He'd already proven that he knew it better than Les did. He made a mental note to keep him better in the loop.

"They may be distracted. I think the Wolvie advance is underway. I could hear it. They're probably in Pine Rapids right now."

Winnie blanched. Pine Rapids was only half-an-hour from Fox. Just up and down the grade. It would take the Wolvics longer to make it to Fox, of course, but it was still close.

Miklos' eyes flashed, and he gripped his shotgun tighter.

He's eager for this. I need to rein him in.

"I could see smoke across the river. They're advancing up both sides. That might be a good thing for us."

"How is that good?" Winnie asked.

"They can't focus all of their forces on this side of the river. They have to spread out their supporting arms."

"How many are coming up at us?" Miklos asked.

"I don't know," Les admitted. "Could be a company, could be a regiment. I'm guessing a battalion, though. About nine-hundred troops," he added when he saw neither knew how many were in a battalion.

"Like I was saying, though. They might be distracted. The team will be providing overwatch to the Wolvies in Pine Rapids. If we can close with them quickly, we can get in range. But that's where I need you two.

"My MEW needs time to recycle. Maybe fifteen seconds."

That is if it is still working right after all these years.

Les mentally kicked himself in the ass. He should have tested it out before this. But if the recharging relay didn't work, then he'd have wasted what would have been his only shot.

I just have to pray you're up to the task, he thought as he gave the stock a pat.

"I need you to come with me when I make my charge to close the distance."

Miklos' eyes lit up, and a half-smile crooked the side of his mouth. It wasn't a happy smile, but more of a predator's.

Winnie just looked at him, her face blank, as she listened.

"As soon as I fire, we all need to take cover. I need you to make some noise, to fire your weapons. You don't have to expose yourself. Just shoot and keep them guessing. As soon as I'm recharged, I'll engage."

Lieutenant Jorgenson, his platoon commander when he first became a platoon sergeant, would have raked him over the coals for such a short mission brief, but sometimes, in the heat of the action, that was all there was time for.

"And if they spot us first?" Winnie asked.

"We take cover, and I'll figure out a way to get closer."

"They won't spot us," Miklos said with conviction. "We'll make them pay for Suki."

Les opened his mouth to say something, then closed it. Miklos had to have his head in the game if they were going to have a chance, and blinding anger resulted in mistakes, mortal mistakes. He understood the loss that Miklos was feeling, but at the moment, he didn't have time for a long heart-to-heart. He just had to hope for the best.

The three hugged the side of the rock face as they moved forward. Les stopped them just before they came into sight of the team.

"One at a time, get on your belly and crawl forward until you can just see the ground. Pick your path. The Wolvies are under the grey vein in the rock. Whatever you do, don't stand up and don't use your weapons," he told both of them, even if he was specifically addressing Miklos. "You've got thirty seconds each."

It was entirely possible, even probable, that they'd all pick the same path over the ground, but it was better that they each get a look instead of blindly running around the edge of the rock face. Any hesitation could be the difference between getting off the first shot and not.

After each of them had gotten a look, he gave them a last check, making sure their weapons were off safe, that their shoes were tight. It wasn't the full inspection he'd given his troops over the years, but it was going to have to do.

"Ready?"

The two nodded, clearly excited. The look on Miklos' face stopped him. Maybe he'd been too short in his brief after all. The guy was getting ready to yell.

"We keep quiet until I fire. No yelling. Nothing. Understand?"

Miklos closed his mouth with an embarrassed look. "Yeah, yeah, I got it. Sorry."

Les patted him on the shoulder and said, "Then let's go."

He sprinted forward past the edge and turned to follow the rock face. He had to focus on his footing, but he kept glancing up to where the disc-recon team was. At any moment, he expected to see the cloaking fracture as they took the three of them under fire, the last thing his brain would register before their rounds cut him down.

Twenty, thirty, forty meters . . . Les wondered if they'd displaced until he caught the slightest of shimmers. They were still there, and unbelievably, they hadn't noticed the three of them running up from behind.

Disc-recon were the best of the best in the Wolvic Army, and Les had feared this was a suicide mission. As he got closer, he began to hope that their mad attack might actually succeed. He started to bring up his MEW, but he needed to be just a little closer. It was imperative that he take one of them out with the first shot. He couldn't afford to have to go through two recycles. He was counting on the surviving Wolvic to be momentarily confused after his first shot, reacting to Winnie and Miklos, enabling him to get off a second shot. But if he didn't get a kill with that shot, they'd realize what was going on and who was the real threat the moment he fired again. Beam weapons had huge signatures that were impossible to miss, and his beam going out was an arrow pointing back at him.

Twenty more meters. That's all I need.

There was another shimmer ahead of him.

Is that one of them turning around toward us?

He couldn't take the chance. He'd been carrying his MEW in the assault position. He'd been deadly with it before losing his arm and having to switch sides, but at this distance, it shouldn't matter. Les fired a sweeping one-second burst, a bolt of lightening delivering gigajoules of death. The beam impacted on bare rock, but his sweep touched one of the cloaking bubbles, which shattered in a blinding flash.

Les didn't wait to survey the damage. He ducked behind a rock while behind him, Winnie and Miklos dove for cover. Winnie immediately fired up into the air, but Miklos, who had taken cover just eight or nine meters away from Les, to his right and slightly forward, popped up and fired his shotgun toward the second soldier.

"Get the hell down!" Les yelled a moment before hypervelocity darts peppered the rock Myklos had just ducked behind, sending dust up in the air.

Miklos turned his head to Les, his face flushed, and said, "I had to give him a target."

Stupid fool, Les told himself, but with a small laugh.

He looked down at his MEW, trying to will it to recharge. The lights were flashing, but that didn't mean power was flowing. He regretted having to fire a one-second burst, the longest a MEW was capable of, but if he hadn't, he'd have missed them.

Winnie and Miklos kept up their firing, and more darts peppered the area. A couple were too close, and Les pulled his legs in tighter. He didn't know if he'd been spotted or if the Wolvic was just trying to blanket the area.

His MEW was still flashing red when a familiar, and frightening buzz reached him. He looked up, raising his still uncharged MEW. The big gun wasn't the best weapon in the world to take out a Mosquito, the Wolvics anti-personnel minidrone, but he had no choice. Without body armor, the Mosquito would kill each of them, one after the other, while the Wolvic soldier kept them pinned.

He caught movement as the hornet-sized drone reached them, but his MEW was still red. A Mosquito fired single darts, a tiny AI selecting the best place to target to reach human flesh. Les switched his MEW to the widest aperture and raised the weapon, ready to fire the instant it was recharged

The movement was picked up by the Mosquito, and he could see the tiny thing, just five meters away, start to turn toward him.

Les desperately pushed the firing stud over and over, but nothing happened. He could see the Mosquito lock on and was about to try and roll away when Miklos fired, and the Mosquito exploded into a cloud of tiny particles.

Just beyond the destroyed Mosquito, Miklos was grinning wildly at him, his shotgun still raised. Les gave him a relieved thumbs up when Miklos' rock was hit again, but this time finding flesh. Miklos yelled and ducked back, holding his left forearm. He'd let it stray out too far to kill the Mosquito and paid the price.

He grimaced as he examined it, then looked over at Les and returned the thumbs up.

Les looked back down at his MEW, but the damned lights were still running red. It looked like the old weapon was beyond its shelf date. He had to go to Plan B . . . except he'd never thought Plan A would get this far, so he didn't have a Plan B.

He had to see what he faced. With the surviving Wolvic firing at them, their cloaking would be compromised. He shifted around to pop his head around his rock when the glorious sight of a small, green LED greeted him.

"I knew you could do it, girl!"

He glanced at the power level: 72%. That last shot had used up a good chunk. He debated narrowing the aperture to save energy, but he hadn't seen the enemy soldier yet. These were the best soldiers in the Wolvic army, and he'd be able to react quickly the instant Les exposed himself.

With regret, Les dialed to the same aperture as he had for the first shot.

He took three calming breaths, the rose to a steady kneeling position, triggering the MEW before he even spotted the enemy soldier, then swiped it across toward him.

In the instant before the beam hit the deadly-looking man, the soldier seemed to realize what he faced, and knowing it was too late, tried to duck. The beam hit him in the shoulder, and his body boiled from the inside, quickly enough for it to essentially explode, the mist of blood and body parts cooking in mid-air before the beam cut off.

Les stood, sweeping the muzzle of his MEW, looking for a target. But both soldiers were down, their bodies ravaged by the meson beams. The Wolvic disc-teams were generally two people, but experienced soldiers knew never to assume that the enemy was going by their SOP. He looked to the side, trying to catch the shimmer of another cloaking bubble. There was nothing.

"You OK, Miklos?" he asked while he scanned the area.

"Yeah. Just a nick," he said, his voice tight.

"You saved my ass there," Les told him.

Miklos just shrugged, his right hand clamped over his left forearm. Blood seeped from between his fingers.

"Winnie? How about you? You OK?" he called over his shoulder.

"Did we . . . did we win?" she asked.

"Hell, yeah, we won," Miklos said, standing up.

Les hadn't seen any sign of another Wolvic, so he stepped over to the young man and looked at his arm. There was clean, shallow slice running about 12 centimeters along the top of his forearm. Miklos had been lucky. He'd been scored by one of the fins as the dart passed by. It was bleeding heavily, however. Les tore away Miklos' sleeve, pulled out a pressure patch from his first aid kit, and pressed it against the slice, holding it as he counted to ten before releasing it. He'd had the patch for years, but it latched onto the skin.

"Man-oh-man," Winnie said as she stepped up to him, leaning forward to look at his arm. She touched the patch. "Does it hurt?"

That might seem like a stupid question given Miklos had been shot, but hypervelocity darts often cut through nerves so cleanly that the pain was tolerable.

"It's not bad," Miklos said, flexing his fingers. "I'm good to go."

Les hadn't seen any sign of life from the disc-team, not that he expected to, at least from the second one. That had been a pretty graphic death, the type that had stoked fear back in the day before the weapons were phased out. He still needed to check them.

"You two wait here," Les told them as he started walking over.

"I'm coming, too," both of the others said in unison.

Les just grunted. He wasn't going to argue, and maybe it was better than they see the fruits of their labor. And it was the fruits of their labor. Without Miklos, he'd have been killed by the Mosquito. Without Winnie's distraction, the disc-recon soldier might have been better able to react to him.

Les took a quick look down the mountain into Fox, the first time he'd done that since arriving at the rock face. One of the boats was underway, towing one of the hulks, but there still seemed to be too many people at the docks, and others were still in the town proper.

"Get a fucking move on," he snarled, wishing he was down there kicking people's butts.

As he got closer to the Wolvics, he knew he didn't have to worry about the first soldier playing possum. She hadn't exploded as spectacularly as her partner, but there was no doubt she was gone. Half of her head was blackened and charred, the smell of cooked meat reaching out to them like a Landing Day BBQ.

Winnie faltered a few steps behind him, but a moment later, she strode on. Les gave a tiny nod of respect. He'd been more than a little queasy the first time he'd been in a firefight, and as the boot, been ordered to search the dead enemies' clothes.

A set of parse-binos stood on a stand just past the body of the first soldier. Les ignored the bodies and stood over the binos. Down below, he could see movement coming out of Pine Rapids. He knelt behind the binos, and the town came into sharp focus. A line of armored cars was leaving the town along the highway. Displayed on the bino screen were the targets, each with a numerical designation. The soldier in him noted the positions. He agreed with some of them, but thought the Fire Support Coordinator missed some of the more obvious spots from which a Capernican force could hit the column—if there was a force available.

"Hey, can we use their disc-thingies?" Miklos asked.

"No. They're coded to their riders, and we don't have the ability to hack them," he answered. "But we need to get moving. The Wolvies are already leaving Pine Rapids."

First, however, he wanted to check a little more. The lower hills and forest blocked the views for most of the next ten klicks, so Les adjusted the cursor to where the first bend in the grade would be visible from their position . . . and froze for a moment. The Wolvics were already there. A TK-12 Basilisk, which was a cross between a tank and an armored personnel carrier, was already rounding the bend, infantry pacing alongside.

How the hell did they get there so quickly?

He looked back to Fox again. He couldn't see as much of the town here as from where he'd looked before, but the docks were in full view. There was still mass confusion down there, with boats at the docks and others waiting for their turn.

He shifted one more time to the binos, zooming in. Another vehicle, this time a PK-80 Warg armored personnel carrier, followed the first around the bend. If they managed to get this far this fast, then they'd be in Fox within the hour, and that was at the infantry's pace. And from the looks of things, there would still be townspeople waiting to evacuate.

Les stood back up and said, "We've got to move, now!"

Chapter 11

The three covered the ground back to the edge of the rock face in 30 seconds. They had to slow down around the edge, though, to navigate the jumbled scree. Within a couple of minutes, Les was huffing and puffing like a pipe organ and afraid he was going to twist an ankle. He almost fell twice, but somehow, he managed to keep on his feet. His MEW was unbalancing him, as heavy as it was, and while he had the muscle memory on how to run with the big weapon, he no longer had the muscular stamina, and as good as his prosthetic was, it just didn't react as well as his real arm in maintaining his balance.

"Let me take that," Miklos said, coming up from behind him.

Les recoiled. No mudhog ever willingly gave up his weapon. That had been drilled into every soldier since they were recruits. He started to argue, but Miklos, soft-looking, somewhat overweight Miklos, wasn't even breathing hard.

Am I that much out of shape?

He looked at his wristcomp, which he'd set to timer. The seconds were ticking away, and he couldn't let stupid pride get in the way of the mission. He handed his MEW to Miklos, and with Winnie bringing up the rear, they started making better time. They reached the trail, and with bounding, ankle-risking leaps, ran down it. Long before he expected it, they reached his Ion.

Les was still puffing, his lungs on fire, but there would have been no way he could have gone this quickly carrying his MEW. Still, he was happy to get it back and sling it over his shoulder. He and Miklos horsed the bike around.

"Do you want me to drive?" Winnie asked.

For a moment, Les was tempted. The Wolvics might have a screening force protecting the lead element, and he wanted to be ready to engage them. But going down the trail would take some skill, more so that coming up.

"No. I'll take it down to the road. I need you two to run behind me. I don't need you to get me off-balance."

What had taken them twenty minutes to climb took almost thirty to descend. Les was exhausted and aching by the time they reached the first paved road, but the bike was in one piece. Milos and Winnie had kept pace, and Les shifted the MEW to his front to give Winnie room. Once the two of them jumped on, Les poured on the power. They had to get to the Wolvics before the Wolvics got to the town.

Chapter 12

"Get to the docks Miss Tension!" Les yelled, slowing the bike.

"I ain't gonna let no Wolvic chase me away from my home," the old woman said from the chair on her porch. "I already told everyone that."

Lane Tension, always "Miss Tension," had come to Fox in the first wave as a young girl and had been half of the first marriage in the town. She'd lost her husband before Les and Emmeline had arrived, and was now a fixture. Hardheaded, to be sure, but well-loved.

Les' initial reaction was to argue, even to bodily take the woman on the bike and deliver her, but time was too tight. Besides, she was a grown woman, able to make her own decisions. She might be old, but no one who'd ever experienced her biting tongue thought her mind wasn't sharp as a tack.

With regret, Les throttled back up.

"Are we just going to leave her like that?" Winnie asked from behind him.

"Her choice. And we have our mission."

There were other people still in the town, more than he'd have imagined. Several called out to the three, but Les put on mental blinders, ignoring them. There was no time.

He pulled a sharp turn onto the highway, gunning the motor too fast. Without the gyros, that would have put the bike down. But the trusty Ion-6 kept upright and recovered as they surged up the grade. He took the curves and switchbacks faster than he should have risked—the gyros couldn't keep them from going off the edge—but it didn't take long to reach the pass, then start down the other side.

Where are they? How far have they climbed? he wondered, trying to make the calculations. He could query his wristcomp, but garbage in, garbage out. He'd have to be making SWAGs as to the inputs. No, better just to push it and keep on the alert.

They reached the site where the militia had been killed, the smell of cooked flesh smacking them in the face.

"Keep it steady, Miklos," Winnie said. "We need you focused."

Les kept driving, going farther down the grade before slowing down. The bike's motor was silent, of course, but the wind in their face and tires on the roadbed created enough sound to affect his hearing. He brought the bike to a stop and listened. Miklos started to ask a question, but Les raised a hand to cut him off.

The TK-12 Basilisk, which was leading the advance, was fusion-powered, but at 45 tons, it would be making far more noise than his Ion as its esterpolythene tracks stressed the road. And he could just hear it coming. They could go a little farther.

He took two more bends, which led to one of the switchbacks. Perfect ambush territory. He turned the bike around so that it was heading uphill, then got off.

"So, here's what we're going to do. Winnie, I want you on the bike. You're driving. Miklos, you're with me—"

"I want to fight, Sergeant," Winnie protested. "I can do it."

"I know you can, but your Brady isn't much of a weapon."

"And Miklos' is? Against a tank?"

"No, it isn't, but it can take out a drone. Now listen. We don't have much time.

"Miklos, you're going to be on my ass. If a drone comes at us, you need to be ready. I'm going to see what I can do to slow the bastards down. As soon as I take my shot, we're going to hightail it out of here and get set to do it again. Winnie, you're driving. I'm next. Miklos, you're our tailgunner."

"Our what?" he asked.

"Sorry. Historical reference. You're going to be sitting on the back of the bike, facing the rear and watching for anything heading our way. Can you do that?"

Milos looked at the bike as he considered it. "If Winnie doesn't gun it, then I think so."

"How many rounds you got?" Les asked.

"Nine. Birdshot."

Shit. I was hoping he had more.

"Don't waste them. Only fire if you've got an actual target, OK?"

"Got it, boss."

He looked at Winnie, who seemed upset. As a leader, he understood that. She'd been attached to his hip for the last couple of days, and now she could think he was dismissing her in favor or Miklos. He needed to get ready, but he could spare a few seconds.

Les put his hand on Winnie's shoulder. "Look, I really need you. You've proven you can drive, and I can't be worrying about that. But keep your Brady ready. When the shit goes down, if you see a target, take it. It won't do anything against armor, but a round in the schnoz will fuck up anyone's day. You with me?"

"I got it, sir. Don't worry about me," she said.

Completely out of left field, he had a sudden urge to reply with the age-old saying, "Don't call me sir. I work for a living," but he let it go. There was a time and place for everything, and this wasn't it. He gave Winnie's shoulder a squeeze, then turned around to pick a firing position.

The far side of the switchback was only 120 meters away over the chasm between, whereas the route on the road was close to 900 meters. If he could hit them hard and make them deploy their infantry, he could slow them down for ten minutes, maybe longer while they figured out just what they faced. Ten minutes was much in the grand scheme of things, but maybe they could get out another boat or two in that period of time.

Les went prone right at the inner edge of the turn. He flipped up the bipod and settled in. With the road bending to the right, this was one case where firing left-handed was an advantage—most of his body was canted back under the cover of the hill. There was another related advantage. Anyone who's fired prone on rocks or a road knows the pressure it puts on the supporting arm's elbow. Les' supporting arm was his prosthetic. It was fairly high-tech, and he could "feel" all along its surface, but that was not translated as pain.

I'll take whatever advantage it'll give me, he thought as he twisted the beamer to check the readings (the display was meant to be easily read when firing right-handed). Sixty percent. His two shots had eaten a huge chunk of the power.

No getting around it. But now, let's focus the beam.

He dialed in Aperture 1, which was a narrow beam of approximately three centimeters in diameter, give or take. Les had done the math at boot camp, but all he specifically remembered was pi-r-squared. In general, if the beam width was doubled, the power usage was something like quadrupled for the same strength beam.

"You ready?" he asked Miklos.

"Ready."

Les had never been a sniper, but he had lain in wait while in ambushes before. The key was to remain calm, not to let the passage of time build up stress. This time, however, it didn't take long. The sounds of the Wolvic approach became louder, and tiny dust-volcanos rose a few centimeters off the roadbed.

"This is it," he said, settling into position, flipping the trigger cover, his forefinger hovering over the trigger stud itself.

The first sign of anything was a drone that came around the corner. Luckily, it didn't cut straight across to them but followed the road.

"We've got one drone," he told Miklos. "It's a Dragonfly. Heavier than the Mosquito you knocked down, but your birdshot might be able to handle it."

Twenty seconds later, the Basilisk rumbled into view. The TK was an older vehicle. The Alpha and Bravo models were fully armored against beam weapons. With the demise of beamers and the infantry level, they'd been updated with their reactive armor that was much more effective against kinetic rounds, but that didn't mean they were completely vulnerable to weapons such as his MEW. They weren't heavy tanks, but they still were pretty protected.

Given enough power and good, accurate shooting, Les could probably take out the tracks or the exterior weapons control. But in this case, to his relief, he didn't have to do that. As he was hoping, the commander was riding with his head out, surveying the scene. He was wearing a full helmet with visor, so he was protected from most small arms . . . but not a MEW.

In his eagerness to engage the commander, he almost missed another small helmet, lower on the vehicle—the driver. That surprised him. Like all armor, Basilisks had an autodrive function, complete with AI interface. But if the driver was in his seat, then the tank was on manual. Which didn't make sense. Unless they didn't trust their autodrive on a mountain road?

Les wasn't going to argue. He lowered his MEW sights and put the crosshairs on the helmet of the driver as he horsed the Basilisk around the curve. At this range, with a beamer, there was no leading, no taking wind or drop into account. It was point and shoot.

A tenth-of-a-second beam shot out, and the driver's head exploded. With his hands relaxing on the controls, the vehicle corrected to the last heading . . . which was right off the cliff.

The commander leaned over to see what had happened and took in the bloody mess of what had been his driver. Les could see him recoil, then shout into his mic as the front of the TK reached the edge of the road. He'd be trying to reimplement autodrive, and the two sets of treads started to reverse, but it was too late. Gravity was a mother fucker, and it had its fingers latched onto the big piece of armor. The edge of the road broke away, and the 45-ton vehicle slid over. Les risked raising his head to watch it roll down the slope, flattening trees in its path.

No time to enjoy your handiwork, Baptiste!

"Go, go, go!" he shouted, getting up and rushing to the Ion and jumping behind Winnie. A split second later, Miklos landed behind him. Les' feet quested to the pegs, but the younger man had latched the front of his ankles around them so he could face backward and not fall off. Les ceded the pegs to him and spread his legs as Winnie took off.

Miklos fired his shotgun, then shouted, "I got the bastard, I think. It went down, at least."

Les hoped Miklos was right, but he doubted it. Dragonflies were tough drones, and it would have had to be close for Miklos' birdshot to have an effect.

Winnie accelerated the bike through the next two switchbacks, pulling over close to the hill. Les stepped off and went back to pick a firing position. This switchback wasn't as good an ambush site as the first, but it would do.

Les looked back, hoping he could see something, but the curves of the mountainside hid the last position from him. However, to his surprise, he had a small window to where he could see farther. The curve before the last site jutted slightly into view, and infantry were advancing below the lip of the road on the slope itself.

Les aimed his MEW and triggered the rangefinder: 826 meters. He could bump up the power and drop a grunt at that range, but to what end, other than depleting his dwindling power?

But he could fuck with them.

"Winnie, bring me your Brady," he said over his shoulder. The small-caliber weapon might not pack a big punch, but it had more than enough range to reach that far.

"What do you want?" she asked.

"We've got a few infantry in sight. I think we need to remind them that we're here."

He held out his hand for the rifle, and she gave it, albeit hesitantly. Her brows were furrowed, and she looked like she wanted to say something, but was biting it off.

Hell, of course. Here, I'm doing it again.

"Give me a good prone position," he told her.

"What?"

"If you're going to take the shot, you need a good prone position. Unless you don't want to, of course."

Her eyes lit up, and she almost jumped onto her belly. "No, no! I want it."

"Oh, man," Miklos said. "She gets to?"

"Now, you see those mudhogs down the slope? I've got them at eight-twenty-six meters. It's a long shot, but within range. I don't care if you hit one or not. Just make them take cover, OK?"

"I've got them," she said eagerly, as she settled in.

Les tried to remember the specs on the Brady's .288 rounds, but was coming up blank. He had to trust the rifle's processors.

"The microgyros will try to guide you, but it's your call. I'm guessing your aim point will be about a meter high at this range, and with the breeze coming up from the river, about ten centimeters left."

She waited a moment, then said, "That's about what it's trying to tell me."

"Then let it guide you."

"OK. What now?"

"Fire, of course. Shoot the bastards."

"Oh, yeah," she muttered.

The Brady spit out a round, then another. A moment later, one of the five or six mudhogs in sight stumbled and fell while the others scrambled for cover. Two of them hit the side of the slope, right under the lip of the road, weapons deployed aiming up the mountain.

"Uh, it seems like you've still got a couple of targets," he told Winnie. "You might as well give them a shout-out."

Winnie let her breath half out, then pressed the trigger stud again. Les thought he could almost see the vapor trail of the round as it arced to the target, hitting the soldier right in the back. The soldier rolled over, then jumped up and ran up and over the road and out-of-sight.

"Did I miss?" Winnie asked.

"Nailed him. But the armor saved him."

"Probably shit his pants, though," Miklos said.

"And that's all we care about. Make them deploy. Delay them," Les said. "So, let's get ready to give them another punch in the nose."

"A kick in the balls, you mean," Winnie said, still riding high.

"What about the female soldiers?" Miklos asked with a laugh.

"Kick them right there, too," Winnie said, standing up, then returning Miklos' high-five.

Les smiled as he watched them. He'd been that way once, young and dumb. Invincible. Fearless. The three of them would probably not live out the hour. The difference was that he knew it. He understood the situation. They probably knew it at some level as well, but joking around was easier than contemplating the end.

Les turned back over and set up his MEW. He hoped they'd get at least one more shot off. Every minute delayed could make a difference back in town. Hopefully, Emmeline and little Kris were long gone, but there'd been too many people left when they'd rode up the grade.

"Hey, you think they're gonna shoot at us from orbit?" Miklos asked as he got into position behind him.

"No."

"Why not?"

"Because if they still had orbiting platforms, we'd already be dead."

"What do you mean?" Winnie asked.

"They use them to cover advancing forces. If they were still operational, we'd have been spotted and taken out," Les said, matter-of-factly.

"And you are just telling us that now, Sergeant?" Winnie asked.

"Would it have made any difference?"

"I . . . I guess not," she said, but not sounding too convinced.

Les had thought about telling them earlier, but to what end? This mission was vital, and he was pretty sure, given no sign of orbital bombardment to the south or across the river, that the Wolvic forces didn't have the platforms in orbit, or if they did, they were saving them for the final push, and wouldn't reveal their positions to take out three people on a bike.

"What happened to them?" Miklos asked.

"Don't know," Les said as he sighted in his MEW. "Maybe holding them back. Maybe our Navy took them out."

"Our Navy?" both asked in unison.

"That's what they're there for," he said. "Doesn't mean the counterattack is underway. The Navy's got unmanned missiles they could have launched from half the galaxy away."

"But the counterattack could be underway?" Winnie persisted.

"Could be, but we've got our mission here. So, let's get ready."

There was an awkward silence as the three waited for the Wolvics. Les had hoped for a ten-minute delay, but the time stretched on to twenty minutes, then thirty. That was all to the good, of course, but unexpected.

"Have they given up?" Miklos asked.

"No. They're coming."

But Les didn't understand what was taking them so long. Losing their Basilisk was a blow, but not something that would stop an advance. Not unless the commander was suffering from a bout of over-caution, and officers like that didn't usually rise very high in the Wolvic military.

Les pulled up the map of the highway, studying it and trying to picture the actual layout of the ground. He'd been up and down the highway enough, but not done much exploring off the road.

We hit them here, and that's about two klicks of road. Less than a klick as the crow flies.

He tried to put himself in the Wolvic commander's place, to figure out what he would do. With only three of them opposing the advance, all the commander had to do was roll over them. The Wolvics might take a few casualties, but then the way to Fox would be wide-open.

Unless the Capernicans had a defense in depth . . .

"Shit! Get back on the bike," he yelled at the other two.

To their credit, they didn't question him. Winnie powered the bike up, and Miklos hit the seat right after him.

"Go!" he told Winnie. "I'll tell you when to stop. Miklos, watch above us for drones."

The Wolvic commander didn't know what he faced, so he'd try and find out. If he didn't have orbital surveillance, he did have his organic drones and scouts. A dragonfly had already been knocked out, proving that the Capernicans had teeth, so he wouldn't just send his assets up the highway. He'd send them up the flanks, and the position Les had chosen was open to the rear and from above.

Not just surveillance. He'd get security up on the high ground so if the main column was hit again, he'd hit the ambushers from the flank. Standard tactics.

Winnie pushed the Ion, gobbling up the road while Les hashed out his plan. He knew where they had to make their stand, but he had to have an answer for the flank security. It would probably be the commander's scouts, either four or six disc-mounted troops. Unlike disc-recon, these troops were outfitted to fight.

"Stop at the combs," he told Winnie.

The combs were a series of rock "teeth" on the far side of Thule Meadow, cut by centuries of runoff. The crevasses would give them cover and concealment, yet if the three of them climbed high enough, there was a spot in them that could have decent coverage of the highway for at least 400 meters, both in front of Thule Meadow and beyond. But he had to know where the Wolvic scouts were.

"Full speed to the other side," Les told Winnie as they reached the near side of the meadow. She complied, goosing the bike and almost losing Miklos on the rear. The stink of death still heavy in the air as they zipped by it. He'd originally intended to bypass the meadow, knowing the Wolvics would slow down and ensure the meadow was secure. Now, he couldn't afford to do that.

Winnie turned around and asked, "Here?" as they reached the first of the combs, and Les nodded, stepping off the bike before she'd come to a complete stop.

"I want you two to wait here for me. Watch for any movement on the far side."

He got back on the bike and turned it around.

"What are you going to do?" Winnie asked, but to his back as he blasted it back across to the other side of the meadow, swerving it to a stop.

"Sorry to do this to you," he said, turning on the autodrive and setting "Home" as the destination. He stood there for a moment, trying to work out timelines in his head. Not at all confident of his choice, he set 15 minutes on the control, then took off at a sprint back to join the other two. What started as a sprint turned into a wheezing jog by the time he got there, only 200 meters away. The MEW on his back kept banging him with each step.

"Why did you leave the bike there?" Winnie asked. "How are we going to get out of here?"

"We're not," Les told them.

Winnie and Miklos turned to look at each other, then gave the tiniest of nods. Winnie turned back to Les and asked, "So, what's the plan?"

Chapter 13

"Just a few more steps," Winnie said. "Easy."

Only they weren't nice, even steps, and it wasn't easy. Winnie had scrambled up the rocks like a monkey, but the last 24 hours had taken their toll on him, and Les was beat. He stood a good ten meters beneath her, his chest heaving as he struggled for breath. It was only by thinking of Emmeline and the others that he was able to grit down and push forward, surging the last leg of the climb to reach the ledge. Winnie helped him up, and he had to fight just collapsing on his back.

Now simply referred to as the "ledge," it had been cut years ago, the plans for a restaurant long abandoned with no actual construction finished. It was essentially a hole in the combs, with rock on three sides. There were plenty of signs that people spent time up here: plywood had been placed to cover the open areas between the teeth, and trash, a small stove, and chairs around a makeshift firepit were scattered about. As Les looked around, he could appreciate the vision of the place. It had spectacular potential. On the southern side, he could see the entire Thule Meadows with the waterfall and mountain. In the middle, the Green River flowed into the distance, and on the north side, a good portion of Fox was visible. He stepped forward to get a better look—there were still people at the docks, but not as many as before.

Across the river, Les could see the signs of fighting, getting closer and closer to Little Fork. He gave the town another fifteen minutes before it was overrun. It would take the Wolvics on his side of the river 20 minutes to get to Fox, unless the three of them could slow the advance down. So, Little Fork would fall first, then Fox, not that it made any difference in the long run.

First things first, though. He had to locate the security team that he knew had to be there.

"Ready?" he called out to Miklos, who was already at the far southern corner of the ledge.

"Ready."

"I've got 80 seconds," Les said, looking at the timer on his wristcomp.

All three watched the high ground on the south side of the meadow. True, the flank security could be on the lower slope, below the highway, but the Wolvics hated to give up the high ground as a rule.

Les watched his timer count down, giving a "Ten seconds," as a warning.

Five . . . four . . . three—

At three, his Ion slipped into gear and shot across the highway in front of the meadow. It zipped past below them, and for a second, Les thought he'd wasted his bike, but then a flare on the other side, followed by a whoosh of a shoulder-launched missile, signaled success. They had taken the bait.

The missile came down into the meadow, whipped around the combs not 20 meters below them, then continued down the highway and out of sight. Three seconds later, they could hear the detonation.

A tiny portion of Les' heart cried, but there was no time to think of his bike.

"Did you spot them?" Les shouted. He'd caught the flare in his peripheral vision, but hadn't pinpointed the Point of Origin, the POO.

"Yeah. You were right. They're at the base of the trees you pointed out on the other side," Miklos said.

"Did you see how many there were?"

"No. I just saw the missile take off."

Les hoped it was four, but if the Wolvic commander thought he might be facing a unit of any size, he'd have sent more.

"OK, then, you know where you need to be."

"Got it," he said, then climbed the ladder that led to the top of the combs.

He'd sit at the top, keeping just out of sight, waiting for anyone to fly over. With his shotgun's limited range, he'd need to be close in order to have a chance of doing any damage to a drone or scout.

"Now, it's up to us," he told Winnie.

The two moved to the edge of the center part of the ledge and went prone. With the destruction of his bike—and what he hoped they thought was the enemy—the Wolvic column would probably speed up. He watched down the highway, waiting.

"I'm sorry I got you into this," he told Winnie.

"You didn't, Sergeant. I made you take me, if you remember."

There was a long pause, then Les said, "You'd have made a good soldier."

"Soldier? No way. This is enough of that for me. Navy all the way from here on out."

Les laughed and patted her shoulder. "Your grandfather would have been proud of you."

"I think he's watching," she said, gripping and releasing the stock of her rifle.

She was putting on a good show of nonchalance, but this was getting to her.

The first sounds of vehicles reached them. This spot didn't have a great field of view on the highway itself, so they couldn't see anything yet, but the Wolvics were closing in on them.

Les' MEW was down to 48 percent, not as much as he wanted, but enough to do some damage. He kept his aperture tight.

"Only fire on the soldiers, not equipment," he reminded Winnie.

"I know. You've told me that a hundred times already."

Back off, Baptiste. You're just nervous. She knows what she's doing.

The first Warg came around the bend, flanked by eight mech troops, four on each side. Les almost reminded her to leave the mech troops alone, but he bit it back. She knew.

The Warg advanced at a good pace, the mechies easily jogging alongside. They reached the meadow and kept advancing, stopping directly below the two of them. A small flock of drones flew over them and past, none reaching the ledge's height.

Stupid Wolvies.

Another Warg rounded the bend, this one with straight-leg infantry flanking it.

So, it's a company, Les realized. Wolvic companies typically had a single mechie squad of eight. He'd been afraid it would be a battalion, so a company was a bit of good news.

The infantry showed more caution than the mechies, something that was endemic to all armies. Mech suits tended to give the wearer a feeling of invincibility, and Les was more than willing to teach them the error of their thinking.

The second section reached the first and stopped, while the first started up again. This was a modified bounding overwatch, but with the mechie team always out in front. It was a logical formation for an advance. The rest of the company would probably be another 500 meters behind.

"When . . . ?" Winnie asked.

"Let the mechie team move out a little and force them to come back. Just a minute or so."

Les looked down into Fox again. There were still too many people there, and there was no way they could all make it away before the Wolvics got there, no matter how long the two of them managed to delay the advance.

Every minute delayed means another boat might get out, so buckle down and kill some Wolvies.

A rumble reached across the water, and Les spared Little Fork a glance. The town was about to fall. And when it fell, would those Wolvics turn their attention to the boats from Fox still in the river?

Focus on what's in front of you.

"Now," he told Winnie, leaning out and targeting the base of the 70mm gun turret of the Warg. He gave it a one-second burn, which would not be enough against a TK-12 or a heavy tank, but this was a personnel carrier. As a hover, it had to be light enough for the impellors to lift the thing, so its armor was not as heavy. Les had watched the Tikermans exploit the Wargs's often enough back during the Sesame Action to know where the personnel carrier's weak spots were.

The Warg fell half-a-meter to the roadbed in a crash, making the infantry dive for cover. Beside him, Winnie started firing.

The Warg could still fire its smoothbore, but it couldn't aim straight up. It was out of the action, for all intents and purposes.

Les shifted to the first section, targeting the rearmost mechie. He goosed the joules and fired at the headpiece. A mech suit was much smaller than a Warg, but it was a far more expensive and better piece of gear. The mechie spun around, his armor protecting him, and raised an arm.

"Get back," he shouted and pulled Winnie from the edge. A moment later, the entire side of the combs erupted as hypervelocity rounds peppered it. Rock dust rose into the air, coming in through the opening.

Les risked a quick look, but instead of returning to help the soldiers in the overwatch position, the lead element had sped up. In a moment, they would be out of range. Ignoring the risk, Les upped the joules again and fired, targeting the same mechie. This time, the mechie fell as the meson beam burned through.

"Shit, shit, shit! They're running to Fox!"

Les opened the aperture and leaned over the edge, sweeping a beam over the infantry. At least four exploded as their cells burst.

"Here they come!" Miklos yelled from his ladder.

Les turned to look, just catching a glimpse of four disc-soldiers flying over the meadow, guns laying down fire on the top of the combs. As they flew over the combs, Les lost sight of them. Miklos did not.

There were four shotgun blasts, then Miklos yelled out, "That's right, you bastards. I got two of you."

"Get back down, Miklos!" Les shouted, getting up and running to the other end of the ledge.

"No, no, you fuckheads. I'm here! I'm the enemy! Come get me!" Miklos screamed.

Les saw Miklos' feet disappear as he scrambled out and on top of the combs. Miklos fired off his shotgun, screaming incoherently, when a fusillade of automatic rounds poured down the ladder, followed by Miklos, who landed with a thud on the rock floor. Blood poured from a dozen wounds, but Les thought he saw the young man turn his head, look at him and smile.

"Miklos!" Les shouted, stepping forward as another burst of rounds poured in through the opening, making mincemeat out of Miklos' body and sending rock dust and particles flying, peppering Les. He jumped back, but the rounds had stopped.

"Are you OK?" Winnie asked.

Les wiped the dust from his face, but his hand came back bloody.

"I'm fine," he said, anger threatening to take over him.

Miklos was just a kid, and now Kris was an orphan. There was no excuse for this bullshit. The Wolvics couldn't hope to take the planet, so as the heads of state played chess, the pawns suffered.

More rounds came down the other opening to the top as the disc soldiers tried to clear the ledge. There was at least one of them still up there, and they weren't going to give up.

Les dialed his aperture to wide, walked to the edge of the open front, and yelled, "Come and get us, you bastards!"

They came. Two discs swung over the top of the combs and down the front face. Maybe the soldiers thought they would be facing another shotgun. Maybe . . . Les didn't care about maybes. All he knew is that they didn't expect a ME2 MEW. With one sweep through the air, Les fried the two soldiers. They crumpled in their harnesses while the discs themselves smoked and spun to the ground.

Les turned the MEW over to the display, and as he'd figured, the power was gone. There wasn't enough left to heat a cup of coffee.

"I'm out," he said.

"So am I," Winnie added.

He dropped the useless MEW to the rock floor, his shoulders slumped. They'd tried, but failed. In a few minutes, Fox would be hit. He'd like to think that the Wolvics wouldn't indiscriminately kill those still there, but after what they did to Brookstone . . .

These weren't the same Wolvics he'd fought beside. He didn't know what had happened, what had perverted their sense of right and wrong. Maybe it was because they knew their fight was a lost cause. Still, that was no excuse.

"What now?" Winnie asked, looking uncertain.

"That's it. We tried," he said, his mouth full of rock grit and dust.

He worked up some saliva and spat over the edge of the ledge. "That's about the worst we can do to them now," he said bitterly.

He looked around, just wanting to collapse and sit in his misery, but Winnie was still looking at him expectantly, waiting for him to get them out of this mess.

She was young, too young, and he regretted letting her get involved. She should have been on one of the first boats out. Let her enlist in the Navy and punish the Wolvic bastards who invaded the planet.

Snap out of it, old man!

There was shouting from below, and rounds pinged the roof of the ledge. Any moment, they'd be sending up Mosquitos or grenades.

"Let's get the hell out of here. We can figure out what to do once we get some distance between us," he said, pulling Winnie by the arm. They ran to the second ladder, away from

Miklos' pulverized body, and started to climb up. Les stopped at the top and slowly stuck his head out.

He was just about to climb out when movement caught his eye.

"Get down!" he shouted, almost knocking Winnie off the ladder. He ducked as rounds impacted all around the opening. Winnie shot down the ladder with Les right behind her.

"Four disc-soldiers were waiting for us. Stupid, stupid, stupid," he remonstrated himself.

Winnie was breathing heavily, her eyes darting back and forth.

"I . . . I'm sorry, Winnie. I don't think . . ." he started, then trailed off. He didn't want to say what he thought out loud. In a few moments, the disc-soldiers would come around to the opening, and there would be no place to hide. They were truly fucked.

Les stepped closer to the opening. Down in Fox, people were running in panic. They must have spotted the Warg and mechies coming down the grade. He couldn't see the Wolvics, but he could hear the faint sound of firing.

"You should have left earlier," he muttered.

Les wondered about Miss Tension. She'd still be sitting on her porch, he knew, refusing to leave even with the Wolvics shooting up the town.

A streak over the far side of the river caught his attention. He'd wondered where the Wolvic air was, but it looked like they'd been holding it back in reserve. The streak dipped down toward Little Fork, but it missed the town, firing long.

"Look at that!" he crowed to Winnie. "The idiots are firing at their own . . ."

He stopped as one of the planes inverted, revealing the telltale twin atmospheric stabilizers . . .

"Shit, they're Air Force fighters! Not Air Guard. Confederation Air Force!" he shouted, jumping up and down as another flight swept down from the sky, tearing up the

Wolvic force. Flames billowed, the reflection lighting up the river's surface.

"Are they coming here?" Winnie asked, hope breaking through her voice.

He'd seen two flights, typical Air Force doctrine. They'd come in fast, and would now be climbing to suborbit. They could come back and sweep this side of the river, but whoever had given them the mission had felt the eastern side of the river was the biggest threat. They would hit that column again. Even if they were diverted to thir side of the river, that would take time, time neither of them, nor those still in Fox, had.

No, they wouldn't be coming here. Not soon enough, that was.

The fighters would be the vanguard of the Confederation force, and within hours, the Army would be landing. Capernica would be freed, the invasion crushed. Fox and Little Fork had a love-hate relationship with more than a little jealousy and rivalry, but at least Little Fork was saved, and Les was glad of that. He just hoped that enough Fox citizens had made it out to rebuild the city. Emmeline would see it happen, even if he didn't.

As he looked across the river, two disc-soldiers dropped over the top of the combs, swooping down to the ledge opening. One of the soldiers pointed to them, and the two started crabbing to position themselves. They had to have seen the Air Force strike on the other side of the river. They had to know they were doomed, but from the look in their eyes, Les knew they were not done. They wanted to kill the upstarts who had managed to take out the other disc-soldiers.

And Les understood it. He'd lost friends in battle, too, after all.

There was no place for the two of them to go, and the disc-soldiers knew it. They were going to take their time, to make sure he and Winnie knew who'd killed them.

Winnie stepped up beside Les, her arms going around his waist. Les put his arm around her shoulders as he stared

Jonathan P. Brazee

defiantly at the two soldiers as one of them gave the two Capernicans the finger . . .

. . . as a blast of flame swept the disc-soldiers from the air, the concussion throwing Les and Winnie back against the rear wall and into oblivion.

Epilogue

Les opened his eyes with a force of will. He hurt, and not the ache of aging, but of having his body abused. He turned his head and saw Winnie crumbled in a heap; her body bent in two.

"No!" he croaked out as he struggled to get to her. But she was breathing, strong and sure.

Relieved, he sat back down to clear his mind. As he did a self-assessment, he was pretty sure he had a concussion as well as a broken wrist, and his back was a morass of pain. He crawled to Winnie and gave her a quick survey. She had a gash on the back of her head that had bled profusely and another on her hip, but she didn't look in distress. He straightened her out and tried to brush some of the dust off her face.

Les was surprised they were alive. They'd been blown back with tremendous force, all the way to the rock wall that made the back of the ledge. As he didn't think the Wolvics had blown themselves up, there was only one logical conclusion as to what had happened. There had been another flight of Air Force or even Navy fighters, and that one had targeted the west side of the river. As if he needed much more evidence, two flights were a pretty good indication that the Confederation military was here in force. The nightmare was going to end—but not before too many lives were lost.

"Are we still alive?" Winnie asked in a little-girl voice, looking up at him with a confused expression on her face.

Bloody and covered with dust, Les thought that was funny and broke out laughing, more in relief than anything else. He hugged her and assured her that they were alive. But if they were alive, what about the Wolvics? Were there any other survivors?

Les stumbled to the opening and looked out. Below them were the remains of the Wolvic force. He didn't think there was anything larger than a baseball left. It was evident that no one had survived. He and Winnie had been lucky, protected by the mountain itself.

Les looked down the highway for the rest of the force, but saw nothing other than a few wisps of smoke rising from around the far bend. If he was a betting man (and he'd been known to make a wager or two), he'd bet that the smoke was rising from what had been Wolvic infantry company.

Shit, what about Fox?

He swung back around, stepping to his left to get a better view. At first glance, the town seemed OK, but those were the homes and buildings closest to the river. The bulk of the town was not in sight.

Several boats were still at the dock, and there were a few people moving about.

"We need to get down to Fox," he told Winnie. "You up for that?"

She rose unsteadily, putting her hand out to the wall for support. "What about Miklos?" she asked, tilting her head to the dust-covered remains.

If Les squinted, they might be a piece of discarded carpet or a bag of trash. But he knew what they were. Miklos, with his wife torn from him, had tried to divert the disc-soldier's attention from them, and it had cost him his life. Les was sure that he'd intended to die from the moment he insisted on coming with them. He'd hoped that having little Kris would have been enough of an anchor to the living, but in the end, losing Suki had been too much.

I shouldn't have let him come.

But I'd be dead now, and the Wolvies wouldn't have been delayed. Who knows what would have happened had they gotten to Fox an hour ago?

"We can't take him now," he said, not pointing out to Winnie that the body couldn't be carried, as torn up as it was. They needed a body bag. "We'll come back and pick him up later."

She looked like she was going to argue, but she gave in and followed Les to the same shaft they'd used to climb up. If climbing had been difficult for Les, going down had been worse. His entire body protested, and with a broken wrist, he had minimal use of his left hand. He was sure his arms and legs were going to give up, and he'd fall. Somehow, however, the two managed to reach the ground in one piece. Picking their way through the dead Wolvics, they started the long hike down the grade, but not before Les grabbed a relatively undamaged Wolvic Kyberblade. The Wolvic weapons were coded to each soldier, so the 15-centimeter commercial blade was at least something he could wield. It wasn't much, but he'd felt a little more comfortable with it in his prosthetic hand.

As they trudged down the grade, the extent of the damage became clearer. At least a third of the town was destroyed, and as they reached the Bluejay Street turnoff, they left the highway to see if there was anyone there who needed help.

Les and Winnie surveyed the "heights," the neighborhood farthest away from the river. Most of the homes there were kindling or smoking ruins. Miss Tension's home was gone, just a hole in the ground. Les hoped the stubborn old woman had changed her mind and left, but he was pretty sure he was looking at her grave.

Several bodies littered the area, a few burnt, but others somewhat whole. Les didn't have the heart to check to see who they were right then.

The remains of the Warg and Mech suits were scattered around the area. They had been taken out by the Confederation fighters, that was pretty clear. What wasn't clear was whether the Wolvics had destroyed the neighborhood or had the fighters. Looking at the extent to the damage, Les had his suspicions, but he didn't really want to know.

Not that he blamed the Air Force. Things like this happened in war, and if taking out the entire neighborhood saved more lives, then it was an unfortunate, if necessary, sacrifice.

Maybe it was the Wolvics, though, he told himself. *Better if it was, although it's a moot point for them. Dead is dead.*

He sighed, and with Winnie in tow, started toward the part of Fox still standing.

There were a few people here and there, walking around as if zombies. A few looked up at the two, then ignored them.

"Hey, you two, are you OK?" a loud voice shouted out to them.

A drop-troop, still in his glidesuit, came jogging up, the caduceus of a medic on his collar.

Les started to wave him off, but Winnie said, "He's got a broken wrist."

There were other people who probably were worse off, but once an Army medic had you in their sights, they were like bulldogs. He let the medic do a quick survey, slap on a temporary air-splint, and warn him that he had a concussion and would need a follow-up.

He checked Winnie over, patching the gash on her head and hip.

"What's the status of the landing?" Les asked.

The medic frowned and started to say, "I can't really—"

"Master Sergeant Lester Arceneaux, retired mudhog," he interrupted, introducing himself.

The medic looked back at his prosthetic, then around to see if anyone else was within listening range. "We've got them on the run here. We'll be secure by tonight, if we aren't there yet. The Wolvies are putting up more of a fight on the mainland, but I don't expect they'll last long."

"What about the damage? Do you know?"

The medic's eyes clouded over, and he quietly said, "Your provincial capital, Santa Isabella—"

"San Isabella," Winnie said.

"What? Oh, OK. San Isabella. It was leveled."

Les suddenly thought of that second lieutenant he met at the festival, the loggie. Wysoki, she said her name was. She was going to San Isabella. He hoped she was OK.

"Same with White Water," the medic went on. "Crystal Bay, Belfast City, and Brookstone. They got hit bad."

"Belfast City?" Les asked.

"Razed. I'm hearing everyone dead. You got relatives there?"

"No, not really."

But Little Kris Nagy did. An orphan twice over now.

"I'm glad for that. Tough break."

"Any word on when we can expect more help here?" Les asked.

The medic was part of a drop-troop team, probably four people, sent to give immediate medical care and assess the area. They would not be able to do much more.

"I can't tell you. My team still has to get up to Listeville today, but I'd hope we'd be landing CCTs by tomorrow. Maybe Friday. But don't quote me on that."

Les had never worked closely with Civil Affairs before, who sent out the Civil Contact Teams, and while most grunts tended to dismiss them out of hand, Les had seen the results of their efforts and knew what they could offer, and he'd be grateful for their help.

"Look, you're concussed, Master Sergeant, and you're going to need an x-ray and a real cast. I have to keep sweeping the area, but I need you to go to the aid station we've set up down at the docks. I want you checked out.

"And you, young lady, you're going to need to get those cuts taken care of," he told Winnie. "And you're both going to need a broad-spectrum antibiotic regimen. I don't know what all you picked up in all the dirt."

Les almost laughed at the way Winnie bristled at "young lady." He guessed she'd earned the right to do that.

The medic didn't seem to notice. "Can I get you two to do that for me?"

"Yes, you can, Sergeant," he said, grabbing Winnie before she said anything. "You go do what you need to do."

"OK, I'm serious. You need to be checked," he said, shaking their hands before spotting someone else.

As soon as the medic was checking over Lara Wu, who'd just aimlessly wandered by, Les turned and headed down to the river, Winnie following. But he stopped on Robin Street and turned left instead of continuing to the docks.

"Hey, that's not the way to the docks," Winnie said.

"You go ahead, if you want. I'm going home to get cleaned up.

And wait for Emmeline.

Winnie watched him for a few seconds, then shrugged and followed.

Robin Street didn't look bad. There were broken branches in the road, but the homes looked basically undamaged. His own home, up ahead, looked fine from a distance.

"What the hell?" Les said as he and Winnie stepped into his front yard.

"Oh, my God!" Winnie said, running over to his Ion-6, or what remained of it. "How did it . . . I mean, look at it!"

Les was in shock. He'd seen the missile lock on the bike, he'd heard the detonation. The missile had obviously hit his bike. The damage was extensive. The handlebars were gone, along with all the controls. The seat was shredded, and the rear tire was down to the rim. Yet there it was, somehow obeying his last input, to go home.

Les slowly walked up to the bike and ran his hands over the frame. The paint was gone, with just a few traces of the hand-rubbed finish left. He bent over to look at the motor. The case was scarred, but it looked intact.

Winnie was softly laughing and shaking her head. With half of the town in ruins, with residents dead, this stupid bike was a breath of fresh air, of hope.

"I'm going to rebuild her," Les said with conviction. He had no idea if Emmeline was still alive, and his heart had taken permanent residency in his throat as a result, but this was something he could latch onto, something to not forget, but to shift from the emotional morass that had threatened to overcome him.

"Here, help me get it inside," he told Winnie.

"Inside?" she asked with another laugh. "Miss Emmeline's going to kick your ass if you mess up her house."

"I hope she does," Les said as he started to push the bike to the front door. "I hope she does."

****

Les woke with a start. He was in his easy chair, and night had fallen. He pulled up his wristcomp and tried to call Emmeline, but the civilian lines were still down except for a message that the net was reserved for official communications until further notice.

He stretched, then grunted at the pain. If anything, he was sorer than he was after walking down the grade.

A soft snore emanated from the couch where Winnie was sleeping. She had tried to clean herself up, but there were still dirty spots she missed. She looked awfully young now, her face relaxed in sleep.

Young or not, she'd performed well under the most trying conditions. Without her, more people would have died. Not bad for a poolee, not even gone to bootcamp yet.

His eyes drifted to his I Love Me wall. The frame in the middle was empty. Les had left his MEW up on the hill, and now, he wasn't sure he wanted to retrieve it. Maybe he would, or maybe he'd just keep the frame empty.

He might even be in trouble. No matter what he'd done, he'd still broken the law by having the syn-module.

Screw it. Let them court-martial me.

There was a scraping on the outside of the door, which must have been what had awakened him. He stood up, hand reaching for the knife that he'd dropped onto the kitchen table.

The door edged open, and Les went limp, unable to move.

Emmeline cautiously entered, holding Kris in her arms. She saw Winnie, and her brow furrowed until she turned and saw Les standing there. Tears started to flow as she broke out crying, rushing over to him.

Les enveloped the both of them in a bear hug, oblivious of Kris waking and starting to cry. His own tears joined that of his wife's.

"I thought . . . you were . . . I was so scared!" she got out between sobs.

"I know, I know," Les said, stroking her hair with his prosthetic. "But I made it. We made it," he adjusted, pointing to Winnie, who was just sitting up and looking at them. "Miklos didn't."

That seemed to register, and Emmeline pushed back, hugging Kris protectively, back in control of herself.

"He didn't?" she asked. "Then, when all this is over, we need to take Kris to his people in Belfast City."

Les shook his head and said, "We can't."

"What do you mean?"

"One of the drop-troop sergeants told me there is no Belfast City anymore. No survivors, Em."

She took another step back, searching Les' face. He just stood there, silent.

"He's not going to be the only orphan, Em. The government will figure out what to do."

Emmeline looked down at the boy, whose sobs had turned into little rabbit cries, barely audible. She pulled him close and kissed the top of his head.

"No," she said.

"No, what?" Les asked.

"This boy is not going to be shuttled around by the government. We can't do that. We owe Suki and Miklos."

"What do you mean," Les asked, a small flicker of . . . excitement? Joy? trying to catch fire in his heart.

Was she saying?

"I mean, we've always wanted a child. I know we're old, but grandparents raise their grandkids. Why can't we raise a child? This child? As our own?"

She looked at him, her fortitude shifting to fear, fear that he would refuse.

But she was right. Capernica had to come together now, all working for the greater good. Miklos had saved his life. He owed him a life in return.

He took two steps back to his wife and drew her in, this time more gently, not disturbing Kris.

"We'll raise you, little man, and love you. You are the future that will rebuild Capernica."

Thanks for reading *POG*. I hope you enjoyed it. As always, I welcome a review on Amazon, Goodreads, or any other outlet. I hope you will read the other two books in the series, *Conscientious Objector* and *Veteran*. All three books are connected, but they are stand-alone reads.

If you would like updates on new books releases, news, or special offers, please consider signing up for my mailing list. Your email will not be sold, rented, or in any other way disseminated. If you are interested, please sign up at the link below:

http://eepurl.com/bnFSHH

Other Books by Jonathan Brazee

Call to Arms: Capernica
Conscientious Objector
POG
Veteran

The United Federation Marine Corps
Recruit
Sergeant
Lieutenant
Captain
Major
Lieutenant Colonel
Colonel
Commandant

Rebel (Set in the UFMC universe.)
Behind Enemy Lines (A UFMC Prequel)
The Accidental War (A Ryck Lysander Short Story Published in
BOB's Bar: Tales from the Multiverse)

The United Federation Marine Corps' Lysander Twins
Legacy Marines
Esther's Story: Recon Marine
Noah's Story: Marine Tanker
Esther's Story: Special Duty
Blood United

Coda

Women of the United Federation Marines
Gladiator
Sniper
Corpsman

High Value Target (A Gracie Medicine Crow Short Story)
BOLO Mission (A Gracie Medicine Crow Short Story)
Weaponized Math (A Gracie Medicine Crow Novelette,
Published in *The Expanding Universe 3,* a 2017 Nebula Award
Finalist)

The Navy of Humankind: Wasp Squadron
Fire Ant (2018 Nebula Award Finalist)
Crystals
Ace
Fortitude

Ghost Marines
Integration (2018 Dragon Award Finalist)
Unification
Fusion

The Return of the Marines Trilogy
The Few
The Proud
The Marines

The Al Anbar Chronicles: First Marine Expeditionary Force--Iraq
Prisoner of Fallujah
Combat Corpsman
Sniper

Werewolf of Marines
Werewolf of Marines: Semper Lycanus
Werewolf of Marines: Patria Lycanus
Werewolf of Marines: Pax Lycanus

To the Shores of Tripoli

Wererat

Darwin's Quest: The Search for the Ultimate Survivor

Venus: A Paleolithic Short Story

Duty

Semper Fidelis

Checkmate (Originally Published in The Expanding Universe 4)

The Bridge (Originally Published in the Expanding Universe 5)

Golden Ticket (Originally Published in Hope is Not a Strategy)

The Lost One (Originally Published in Negotiation)

THE BOHICA WARRIORS
(with Michael Anderle and C. J. Fawcett)
Reprobates
Degenerates
Redeemables

Thor

SEEDS OF WAR
(With Lawrence Schoen)
Invasion
Scorched Earth
Bitter Harvest

Non-Fiction

Exercise for a Longer Life

The Effects of Environmental Activism on the Yellowfin Tuna Industry

Author Website
http://www.jonathanbrazee.com

www.ingramcontent.com/pod-product-compliance
Lightning Source LLC
Chambersburg PA
CBHW070501130626
46555CB00003B/1111